'The story line is amazing. When you first open the book
it just draws you in and swallows you whole . . . It was
like my hands were glued to the cover!'
Sophie, age 12

'Exciting and nerve-racking'
Harry, age 13

'As adventurous as **Shark Island**. I couldn't put it down.'
Emily, age 11

'The endings of lots of the chapters were real
cliffhangers, which made me want to read on.
This book is fantastic.'
Angus, age 9 and a half

'My favourite character is Hanna because she is
very brave!'
Lottie, age 8

'I have already read **Sea Wolf** one and a half times now
AND I LOVE IT!'
Rebecca, age 11

Other books by David Miller

DAVID
MILLER

*With special thanks to Max Fenton and Andy Deane, who taught me
more about supertankers than I ever wanted to know!*

OXFORD
UNIVERSITY PRESS

Great Clarendon Street, Oxford OX2 6DP

Oxford University Press is a department of the University of Oxford.
It furthers the University's objective of excellence in research, scholarship,
and education by publishing worldwide in

Oxford   New York

Auckland   Cape Town   Dar es Salaam   Hong Kong   Karachi
Kuala Lumpur   Madrid   Melbourne   Mexico City   Nairobi
New Delhi   Shanghai   Taipei   Toronto

With offices in

Argentina   Austria   Brazil   Chile   Czech Republic   France   Greece
Guatemala   Hungary   Italy   Japan   Poland   Portugal   Singapore
South Korea   Switzerland   Thailand   Turkey   Ukraine   Vietnam

Oxford is a registered trade mark of Oxford University Press
in the UK and in certain other countries

British Library Cataloguing in Publication Data

Data available

ISBN: 978-0-19-272902-6

1 3 5 7 9 10 8 6 4 2

Printed in Great Britain by CPI Cox and Wyman, Reading, Berkshire

Paper used in the production of this book is a natural,
recyclable product made from wood grown in sustainable forests.
The manufacturing process conforms to the environmental
regulations of the country of origin.

*This is for Joe, Lotta
and Christopher Yen-Lung
with love*

Contents

1

Missing!

'It's the biggest pearl in the world,' Ned said, his eyes flashing with excitement. 'It's the size of a man's brain and it's worth thousands of pounds—*millions* of pounds probably! Jik's granny, the old magic woman, told him about it before she died. It's called the Moon Pearl and we're going to find it!'

Ned's best friend Jik, the Sea Gypsy boy, gripped the steering paddle of the *dapang*, the little out-rigger boat that was carrying them northwards across the sparkling Sulu Sea, and nodded enthusiastically. 'Then we sell it,' he declared. 'And get dam rich!'

'Dam *stinking* rich!' Ned emphasized.

Ned's sister Hanna, who was sitting next to the mast, stared open-mouthed at the two boys. *A giant pearl!* Why hadn't they said anything about it before?

'It's hidden on an island called *Babi Besar*, which means Big Pig Island,' Ned went on. 'To find it you have to stand in a special spot that only Jik knows about and wait till the full moon rises. The pearl's buried where the first ray of moonlight touches the ground—isn't that right, Jik?'

Jik nodded again. 'Dead dam right!'

Hanna felt a thrill run through her. The boys were talking about treasure—*buried treasure*! It was like something out of a storybook! She tried to imagine what the biggest pearl in the world would look like. Silvery, like the moon, she supposed—which must be how it had got its name. 'So where exactly is this Big Pig Island?' she asked.

'Near to Palawan,' Jik told her.

'But that's miles away! It's in the Philippines!'

He shrugged. 'No dam problem.'

But it was a problem. A big dam problem. In the months since the children had last been together, Hanna had read everything she could lay her hands on about the Sulu Sea and the people who lived there. She knew that the border with the Philippines lay just a few miles off the Borneo coast, and that beyond it was bandit territory, where thieves and pirates ruled. If they crossed into Philippine waters, they'd be sitting ducks, at the mercy of anybody who cared to rob them—or worse. No pearl, however valuable, could possibly justify taking such a stupid risk!

Her excitement vanished as quickly as it had come. 'You've been planning this all along,' she

2

said to the boys furiously. 'You knew you wouldn't be allowed to cross the border. It's way too dangerous! That's why you didn't say anything to anybody before we set out on this trip. Turn this boat round now!'

'Don't be such a wimp!' Ned told her. 'Don't be such a *girl*!'

Hanna glared at her brother. It took a supreme effort to stop herself from hitting him. 'I hate you!' she yelled. 'I hate both of you!'

'The feeling's mutual,' Ned said.

Hanna felt tears prick at her eyes. This was supposed to be a trip to celebrate the three of them being back together again. They would camp on some islands close to the mainland for a few days and swim and sail and fish. They'd made a solemn promise to Mum—and to Jik's dad, who was Panglima—Chief—of the entire Sea Gypsy community—that they wouldn't do anything stupid, or dangerous.

It was a promise that, right from the start, the boys had intended to break!

How she wished she had a phone so she could call somebody to force the little idiots to turn back. To think they were only two years younger than she was! It could have been ten!

She stared around her uneasily. For the first time, they were out of sight of land—up to now

3

there'd always been the comforting bulk of the Borneo coast away to the south-west. Now they were truly alone, and it would soon be night. Had they already crossed the border without realizing it?

The wind, which had propelled them northwards all day, had swung round to the east and faded completely. The sail hung limp and useless. One thing was clear—there was no way they'd ever reach land before nightfall. That meant spending a night at sea, uncomfortably squashed in the bottom of the boat, with no way of cooking any food.

It was the pits, the absolute pits!

Hanna took off her straw hat and mopped her brow. It was so hot! It was always hot in this part of the world of course—they were only a few hundred miles from the equator—but this heat felt different somehow. It felt thick—*oily*—clinging to her skin, sucking the sweat from her pores. Even the sun seemed to have something wrong with it now. It was a strange copper colour, its light dull and heavy.

She glanced back at Jik. He was adjusting the sail, trying to get the boat moving again. He failed, and returned to his seat in the stern. The carefree expression he'd worn on his face all day had gone.

The calm before the storm.

The phrase sprang into her head unbidden. Was that what this weird, hot, windless period was? She'd been reading about storms in the Sulu Sea only the other day. They were very rare, she remembered the book saying, except for three months in the middle of the year—July, August, and September. That was when typhoons sometimes tracked south from their normal route across the South China Sea . . .

Typhoons were like hurricanes, she knew—only worse. Whole villages could be wiped out on exposed coasts. Even big ships sunk without trace.

It was August now.

Mid-August . . .

The *dapang* gave a sudden lurch. A wave had passed beneath it, the first wave of any size they'd met all day.

A second wave followed.

And a third.

Conscious of the beating of her heart, Hanna bent down and opened the locker below the mast. Wedged in behind rolled-up fishing nets and coils of rope, were three lifejackets. They were old and smelly, filled with what felt like hard lumps of wood. But they were better than nothing. She thrust two of them at the boys.

'Put them on,' she ordered.

'You must be joking . . . ' Ned began.

5

But to her surprise Jik didn't object. He slipped his over his head and fastened the straps. He was peering at the horizon. *'Hunus* come,' he said uncertainly.

'Hunus?' Hanna asked.

'Big dam wind.'

She followed Jik's gaze as she secured her own jacket. To the north a dense bank of cloud had formed. It seemed to be resting on the surface of the sea. There was not even the faintest breeze. It was as if the whole world had come to a halt, and was holding its breath; waiting . . .

At last Ned seemed to understand the danger they were in. He scrambled into his lifejacket. 'It's spooky,' he said. 'I don't like it. We've got to get out of here!'

'And how exactly do we do that?'

He glanced up at the limp sail. With no wind, and no engine, they could go nowhere. His face fell. 'I'm sorry, Hanna,' he said quietly. 'We should have stayed back in the islands . . . '

'It's too late to be sorry!' she snapped.

She turned to help Jik. He was attaching a long piece of rope to the plastic bucket they used to store fish, securing it tightly round the rim. 'What's this for?' she asked, puzzled, as he tied the other end of the rope to the bow of the boat.

'*Boji*,' he told her. 'Anchor. When goddam wind start to blow.'

'But I don't understand how a plastic bucket . . .' Ned began.

'Wait. See.' He hurled it overboard.

For a moment or two nothing happened. Then the rope jerked tight and the little *dapang* swung to face the oncoming waves. The bucket was trapping enough water inside it to hold them steady. It was a brilliant idea!

The sea had begun a strange, agitated dance. White-crested breakers seemed to come from every direction at once. Balancing with difficulty as the boat pitched and yawed, the children fought to take down the sail. With a bare mast it was just possible they could ride out the storm. Jik swiftly cut three more lengths of rope—lifelines in case any of them got washed overboard—and lashed them to the bamboo outriggers. Whatever happened to the boat, Hanna realized, as they tied their lines securely round their chests, the big hollow poles would always float. She caught Jik's eye to thank him. He may have helped get them into this mess, but he was showing a lot of common sense now.

As night fell, the swell rose higher and higher. Now it was so dark she could no longer make out the faces of the others. Ahead of them lightning was flickering, and here and there, through ragged gaps in the cloud, a few stars were visible. It must have looked like this at the beginning of the world, she found herself thinking—and would do at the end. Ned was crouched next to her, all his earlier arrogance gone. She curled an arm round him. 'It'll be fine,' she started to say to him. 'I know it will—'

She never finished.

The storm didn't just break, it *exploded*.

Everything disappeared in an instant. It was as if a massive dam had burst and was sweeping everything before it. Hanna clung desperately to the mast as an avalanche of water—spray; rain; it was impossible to tell which—thundered down on top of her.

The tiny boat began to surf madly down into the vast valleys of water gouged out by the gale, before climbing again, higher and higher, to meet each wind-lashed crest. *Dear God, let this not be a typhoon,* she prayed as she fought to keep her grip. *Let this just be an ordinary storm that'll be gone as quickly as it came . . .*

But it was no ordinary storm.

As the wind rose to an unholy shriek, Hanna's hands were ripped from the mast and she was sent tumbling along the length of the boat. Sharp things—paddles, fishing rods, a rusty anchor—gouged at her flesh. She was going over-board . . .

An arm locked on to hers.

It was Jik. He was wedged against the steering paddle, fighting to keep the boat level. She pushed herself up beside him, clutching at the paddle, adding her own weight, her own strength to his.

But where was Ned?

She squinted desperately through the lashing rain. It was impossible to see anything clearly, even when the lightning was at its brightest. She prayed that he was still safe, that he'd managed to cling on with a tighter grip than she had. Was that dark shape hunched under the outrigger poles him, or was it a bundle of ropes that had burst out of one of the lockers?

'Ned!' she screamed. 'Is that you, Ned!'

But her words were swallowed by the wind. There was no way he would ever hear her.

Long minutes passed. It seemed impossible that the typhoon could get any worse—but it did. It threw itself at them like a ferocious beast. Water—countless tons of it—thundered down on top of them. The boat was already half full, floundering rather than floating. It got harder and harder to steer. They were relying totally on Jik's homemade anchor to keep them upright, Hanna realized. It

9

was just a cheap plastic bucket. How long could it stand up to forces like these?

Then the big wave came.

It wasn't so much a wave as a solid black wall of water. It was taller than a house—taller than the tallest building in the world, it seemed to her—as it raced towards them with the speed and sound of an express train. Jik wrenched the bow towards it, but it was pointless. Not even a large ship could survive a wave like this—let alone a tiny, flimsy sailing boat.

Hanna just had time to suck in a lungful of air before the *dapang* swerved sideways, and somersaulted high into the air.

For a second she was flying, but then the wave grabbed her and crushed her into itself, and she was whirling round and round in a mad tangle of spars, ropes, and sails.

Down she went, further and further down into the blackness—until it felt as if her ears would explode and her brain would burst. Then, just when she thought she would never rise again, she was dragged swiftly, painfully back to the surface. As her head broke free of the water, and she gasped in a draught of air, she realized what had happened.

Her lifeline had saved her!

Battling with the swirling surf, bleeding from

numerous cuts, she hauled desperately on the slender rope. It seemed so long! But at last, just as her strength was failing her, she felt the solid push of wood against her hands.

It was the outrigger.

She flung her arms over it, and hung there gasping with exhaustion and terror. More waves followed, vicious, hump-backed breakers that threatened to tear her loose again and send her tumbling back into the depths; but somehow she clung on.

Then—miraculously, wonderfully—she felt the press of a body against hers. A flash of lightning revealed Jik's face, his cheeks stretched tight with fear. He too had used his lifeline to pull himself to safety.

But where was Ned? Why hadn't he joined them?

Groping blindly in the blackness she found his line, still securely tied to the outrigger.

She began to haul it in. At first she thought he must be swimming towards her, because why else would it be so slack?

It was only when she reached its frayed, tattered end—reached the place where the terrible force of the wave had snapped it in two—that the desperate truth became clear.

He was gone.

2

Return to Shark Island

Hanna and Ned hadn't expected to come back to Kaitan—the beautiful tropical island off the coast of Borneo where they'd survived a terrifying pirate attack a year earlier—quite so soon. But then Mum hadn't expected to get the call that had brought them halfway round the world again, either.

It was Sunday lunchtime in the cottage when it came—the first weekend of the summer holidays—and it was raining outside. Hanna and Ned were in the kitchen, helping Dad with the cooking, so it was Mum who picked up the phone in the living room. The conversation was in Chinese, and seemed to go on for ever. Eventually she put down the receiver and came into the kitchen.

'That was my mother in Malaysia,' she announced unhappily. 'My father wants to see me.'

Dad looked up sharply from the potatoes he was peeling. 'He wants to *see* you? Am I dreaming this? What's the old so-and-so up to now?'

'I think he might be ill, but mother won't say.

She wants me to come out to them as soon as possible.'

'She won't tell you what's going on and she still expects you to get on a plane and fly all that way?'

'They're my parents, Nick. I can't just ignore them.'

'Well they've ignored *us* all these years!'

Mum and Dad hardly ever argued, but when they did, it always seemed to be about Mum's parents. She was their only child, and they'd been dead set against her marriage to Dad from the start. Dad had been a hippy when he'd first met her, drifting through the countries of South-East Asia with hardly any money and no regular job— so maybe there *had* been a reason to object to begin with. But not now, not after all this time, not now he was running a successful thatching business back in England. Not now they'd bought their own little whitewashed cottage in Devon with six acres of land; and had two children . . .

Mum's face had gone red. It always did when she was really upset. 'It won't cost us anything,' she said. 'They'll pay for our tickets.'

The children glanced up sharply from the beans they were slicing. *'Whose* tickets?' Hanna demanded.

'They want you and Ned to come with me.'

'No way!' chorused the children aghast.

'Your grandfather has specially asked to see you.'

'We don't care! We *hate* him!'

It was true. They did hate him. They didn't even want to *think* about the sour-faced old man and his downtrodden wife, who'd threatened to have them whipped last time they'd met, and whom they'd only just managed to escape from thanks to a brilliant trick by Ned.

Dad put down his peeler. He was staying calm only with a supreme effort. 'So why does he want to see them after all this time? He's got a nerve to even ask!'

'The kids are his only grandchildren. I think he wants to make his peace with them before he . . . '

'Kicks the bucket?'

Mum's voice choked. 'I hate this!' she shouted, tears filling her eyes. 'I just hate it! I feel torn in half!'

She turned and rushed from the room. They heard her feet on the stairs and her bedroom door slam.

The argument rumbled on all day. Mum won in the end—as she always did—and forty-eight hours later she and the children were saying goodbye to Dad at Heathrow before boarding a non-stop flight to Kuala Lumpur, the Malaysian capital.

In the months they'd been away Ned and Hanna had forgotten about the heat. It wrapped itself around them like a damp, suffocating blanket the moment they stepped out of the air-conditioned airport terminal and into the taxi that would take them to the wealthy suburb of Kuala Lumpur where Mum's parents lived. They'd forgotten about the haze too—the veil of smoke and pollution that sometimes hung over the city, turning everything a dirty grey, and making their eyes water and sting. It was horrible—especially since their *real* holiday—three blissful weeks on the North Norfolk coast where they were going to sail and swim and paddle their kayaks—had had to be cancelled to make way for *this.* They sat sullen and silent, replying only in grunts when Mum asked them questions, or pointed out landmarks as they passed.

But however horrible the city might be, it was nothing compared to the house the taxi eventually pulled up at. It was a squat, ugly building, almost completely hidden by a small forest of gnarled mango trees at the end of a short private driveway. The children had been there before—just once, on their way out to Kaitan the year previously—but Mum's father had refused to open the gates on that occasion, so they had never been inside.

Mum's mother met them at the door. She

seemed to have shrunk since they'd seen her last; bent and shuffling. As they hauled their luggage inside they were hit by an overpowering smell—a stomach-churning mixture of incense smoke, boiled Chinese herbs, and what could only be soiled bedclothes. Trying not to breathe too deeply, they peered around.

The place was in semi-darkness, with all the shutters closed. Angry-faced gods leered down at them from a tall altar-table decorated with smoking joss sticks and plates of oranges. Sinister-looking carved furniture was just visible in the gloom. Mum had grown up here, Hanna found herself thinking. This had been her *home*. No wonder she'd wanted to escape when Dad had come along!

They went into the kitchen, where a frightened-looking maid gave them glasses of sour-tasting water. Mum spoke to her mother for a long time, before turning back to the children. Her face was grim. 'My father's had a stroke. It's quite a bad one—he's paralysed down his left side. He came out of hospital two weeks ago.'

'Why didn't she tell you about this when she called?' Ned asked.

'Mother's very cautious. She didn't want to talk about it on the phone in case it brought more bad luck.'

'That's silly!'

'It's how she is. My father's been asking to see us ever since he got back from hospital. The maid will show you to your room.'

'Are we staying *here*?' Hanna asked, aghast.

'Of course we are! Where else do you expect us to stay?'

'But it's . . .'

'Please, Hanna,' Mum entreated. 'Don't make this any more difficult than it already is.'

But it *was* difficult—and it got more and more difficult as the days passed.

Visiting the old man was the worst thing. He insisted they came to his bedroom every morning. He looked nothing like he had when they'd seen him last. One side of his face seemed to have slipped downwards, and there was a permanent string of dribble hanging from his lower lip. His whole body shook, even though it wasn't cold.

When he spoke, his one good eye fixed them with a laser-like stare, but it was impossible to understand what he was saying. Was he still angry with them? Or trying to be nice? There was no way of telling.

Despite everything, Hanna found herself feeling sorry for him—and for her Chinese grandmother too. They were so old and helpless and unable to cope. But she felt far sorrier for

Mum, who had to lift her father in and out of bed when he needed the toilet, and clean up if he soiled himself.

'Why doesn't he get a nurse?' Hanna asked, after a particularly smelly 'accident'. 'He's got loads of money.'

Mum shook her head tiredly. 'He won't allow anybody except his own family to come anywhere near him.'

'I'd just tell him to lump it!' Ned said angrily.

Mum managed a smile. 'I dare say you would, but that's not the way things are done in a Chinese family. I'm afraid I'm going to be stuck here for quite a while.'

'How long?'

She looked bleak. 'I don't know. As long as is necessary.'

'And what about us?' Hanna asked, appalled. 'Are we going to be stuck here too?'

'I'm afraid so.' She hesitated. 'Unless . . . '

'Unless what?'

Mum paused. A slight smile played at the corners of her lips. 'After you went to bed last night I called Borneo.'

'*Borneo!*' the children yelled.

'The new resort on Kaitan's been open for a few months now. I spoke to Mr Ross the manager and he contacted Jik's dad who said he'd take responsibility for you if you'd like to visit for a few days. You'll have to fly out unaccompanied, of course, but I don't expect that'll be a problem.'

'No problem at all!' yelled Ned, leaping up and down madly, doing the strange, jerky dance he did when he was very excited.

Mum calmed him with an effort. 'I take it that's a yes, then?'

'Yes!' chorused the children.

'But in return you must promise me you won't do anything stupid. I don't want a repeat of last year.'

'But it wasn't our fault!' complained Ned.

'Promise me.'

'We promise,' said Hanna firmly, glaring at her brother.

'What about Jik?' Ned demanded. 'Is he going to be there?'

Mum gave him another of her smiles. 'You'll just have to wait and see.'

Jik wasn't just *there,* he was actually on the runway as the little local plane touched down at Tamu airport on the final leg of the children's journey from Kuala Lumpur. Ned, who had the window seat, spotted him racing towards them as they came to a final stop next to the tin-roofed shed that served as the terminal. It seemed to take for ever for the passengers in front of them to gather their bundles and small children and leave, but at last Hanna and Ned were down the steps and the three of them were together again.

'Holy Moses, you look just the dam same!' Jik exclaimed, after he and Ned had finally stopped capering around giving each other high fives.

'So do you,' Hanna told him.

Jik peered down at himself. 'Holy Moses, do I? I think I am much more dam big!'

She giggled. 'You're a bit bigger. But just a bit!' Holy Moses was obviously the latest Jik-phrase. She wondered how many more there were to come.

The children caught up on all their news as their ancient taxi rattled through the familiar streets of the scruffy little harbour town on its way to the jetty, where the boat was waiting to take them to Kaitan. Jik had spent several months in America, staying with Annie Weir, the professor who'd rescued them the previous year, helping her with her research into the Sea Gypsies. He'd gone to school while he was there, and his English had improved at lot. 'Holy Moses, it's so dam good to see you guys again!' he concluded as they drew up at the quayside.

That was where the first of several shocks Hanna and Ned were to suffer that day took place.

Instead of a *kumpit,* the big, old-fashioned fishing boat they'd been expecting, there was a shiny new speedboat drawn up against the harbour wall. It was decorated with pictures of palm trees and turtles, and had the words *Kaitan Island Resort* painted in huge letters across its side. Kaitan was the Sea Gypsy name for Shark Island. The driver, who was wearing a pair of electric-blue boardies and a string of what looked like sharks' teeth around his neck, was called Jason. He greeted them warmly, and lifted their luggage on board. It was like getting on a bus, not a boat.

The illusion disappeared the moment they nosed out across the harbour bar and into the glistening waters of the Sulu Sea. Jason opened up the throttle and instantly they were thundering northwards in an arc of rainbow spray.

It was so good to be back! And it felt even better when a familiar triangular shape emerged above the horizon. Despite the horror of what had happened there the year before, Kaitan was still the children's favourite place in the whole world. 'The first thing I'm going to do when we get there,' Ned announced excitedly, 'is jump off Dead Man's Leap!'

'Me too!' exclaimed Hanna.

Dead Man's Leap was a special cliff that overhung the lagoon, where the water below was deep enough for you to hold your nose and plunge down and down into it—if you dared!

But Jik was shaking his head. 'Not dam allowed,' he said mournfully.

'What do you mean it's not allowed?' Ned asked, aghast.

'Too dam dangerous.'

'Who says?'

'Mr Ross. He is big dam boss.'

'That's rubbish!' snapped Hanna. 'We've done it hundreds of times!'

'Still not allowed.'

The children's unhappiness deepened further when they finally rounded the corner of the island and swung in through the narrow entrance to the lagoon. The beach was still there—the perfect crescent of white coral sand—and a scattering of palm trees.

But that was about all.

A long concrete jetty split the lagoon in two. Behind it, in the space where their magical creaky hut had been, a thatched restaurant block had been built; and leading from it, on both sides, were the paths to numerous chalets, some close to the beach, others perched high up on the hillside amongst the jungle trees. 'Welcome to Kaitan Paradise Island' a large banner on the jetty read. It looked like a place on a posh holiday programme.

Jik's dad was waiting to greet them. He'd put on weight since they'd seen him last, and had the contented look of a successful businessman. With him was a tall, bronzed white man. 'Hi, kids, I'm Darren Ross,' he said in a loud Australian voice, as they climbed out of the boat. 'General Manager. Welcome to the island—but of course you've been here before! Just a few things to take on board before I show you your chalet.'

He handed the children a photocopied sheet. It was headed: *Let's Keep Our Paradise A Paradise!* It contained a list of twenty rules covering everything from *No noise after ten p.m.*, to *No standing on the coral.* The final rule was heavily underlined: *Positively no jumping off cliffs*.

'Is there anything we *can* do?' Hanna asked coldly, handing back the sheet.

The Australian grinned. 'Yeah. Have a good time!'

Quite how they were expected to do that, she couldn't work out. They couldn't even light a fire on the beach to cook any fish they'd caught—not that they were supposed to *catch* any in the first place. There were notices everywhere saying things like *Take only photos, leave only footprints* and *Respect nature, respect our planet.* It was as though somebody had stolen their precious, untidy, *mysterious* island and turned it into a local park.

23

It wasn't all bad, of course. The reef was still there, as immaculate and wonderful as ever—though they had to share it with the other guests, who seemed to consist mostly of Italian honeymoon couples. And the food was nice—fish brought in by the Sea Gypsy boats every morning; and fresh meat and vegetables from the market at Tamu. There was even hot and cold running water in the chalets, pumped up from the well, which was now hidden beneath a steel and concrete lid.

But it was dull.

Deadly dull.

So dull that when the boys came up to her on the beach one day, grinning at each other conspiratorially, and proposed an expedition to some nearby islands in Jik's new *dapang*, Hanna leapt at the idea.

'It'll be just like old times,' Ned told her excitedly. *'Only much, much better!'*

3

The Ship of Tears

'*Ned!*'

Hanna was screaming his name, howling it into the gale. As each fresh wave picked her up and hoisted her skywards, she peered blindly through the blackness, through the spray. He couldn't have just *gone*! Not Ned. Not her silly, affectionate, infuriating, lovable brother. Not the person who, despite all their fights, was her best friend in the whole world . . .

It was so hard to see, so *impossible* to see, even when the lightning was at its brightest. Ned might have been only a few feet away from her, but she would never have spotted him.

It didn't stop her screaming for him, though. It didn't stop her shouting out his name, long after all sound had gone from her tortured vocal cords.

On and on raged the storm, the wind twisting the sea into crazy whirlpools that threatened to suck her under and hold her down until all the breath was gone from her body. Sometimes she was aware of Jik clinging beside her. Sometimes she was not. As the hours passed and exhaustion set in, a strange feeling of peace came over her. She felt—weirdly—as if she was flying; as if she was hovering above the waves, above the gale, looking down at her own body. Was she dying, she wondered. Was this what dying was like? *'Let go,'* she heard a voice inside her head urging her. *'Just let go. It'll be quick and easy. So easy . . . '*

'Never!' she screamed back. 'Never never never!'

And she was back inside her body again, fighting for her life, her arms almost wrenched from their sockets as the outrigger kicked and bucked beneath her.

Dawn came at last, an angry red glow that seemed to rise up out of the sea like the fire from a distant volcano; and with the coming of the light, the wind, finally, began to ease. Now she could see Jik clinging to the outrigger beside her, his skin stained pink with the rising sun, his eyes closed, his lips moving.

He was praying, she realized—but to whom? Was it Salim, the sea spirit he believed in? He'd dropped coins and rice cakes into the sea before they'd set out, to make Salim happy and ensure a safe voyage.

A fat lot of good that had done . . .

She began to cry. As she did so a thousand voices started crying too, faint at first, muffled by the roar of the waves, but then swelling and growing louder. The whole universe seemed to be crying with her.

As she surfed down the face of yet another wave, she felt a touch on her arm. It was Jik. He was pointing fearfully behind them.

With a painful effort, she twisted her body round. At first she could see nothing except a towering wave-crest.

But then, smashing through it towards them, came a ship.

It was one of the strangest ships she'd ever seen. It was an ancient, wooden fishing boat, with what looked like a scruffy block of flats clinging precariously to its upper deck. It reminded her, weirdly, of Noah's ark.

But instead of animals, it was filled with children—*weeping* children.

There seemed to be hundreds of them, clutching at anything they could find as the ship pitched and yawed in the mountainous seas. It was *their* voices she had heard, Hanna realized—their terrified cries and screams mingling with her own.

As the ship got closer, she could see why.

It was rolling badly, and as each wave hit it, it seemed to tilt over more and more. As she watched, a small boy—he can have been no more than eight—lost his grip and was flung outwards

27

into the swirling waves. She spotted him briefly, his arms flailing desperately, before he was sucked under by the next breaker.

She didn't see him again.

Did anybody on board realize what had happened? The ship must turn round, go to his rescue! She began to wave at it madly, but it didn't change course, ploughing blindly onwards towards them.

She saw with a shock that it was going hit their floating outrigger, smash right into it. They would be dragged under, cut to pieces by its propeller . . .

Jik had realized the same thing. He was fumbling desperately for his knife, which he kept in a sheath on his belt. He pulled it free, and with a quick movement cut the lifelines that bound them to the bamboo poles. Now there was nothing that could save them if they lost their grip. He pointed at the ship. Was he proposing they *swim* to it? Surely not!

Then she understood what he was trying to tell her. Dangling from its side on knotted ropes were half a dozen old motor tyres. They were no doubt used as fenders, to protect the ship's hull when it tied up at a dock. Normally they'd be high above the water line—but not now. As the vessel pitched and rolled, they dragged in the sea. If it didn't change course, and if they got their timing exactly right, there was a chance—just a chance—they

28

might be able to use them to haul themselves on board!

Hanna could read its name now, crudely lettered onto its decaying hull: *The Dreamboat*. It was such a stupid name that normally she'd have laughed out loud. Now it seemed like something out of her worst nightmare.

The cries had risen to an ear-splitting crescendo, intermingled with harsher, deeper shouts. Who were all these children? What were they doing on this floating wreck?

The questions had scarcely formed in her head before the ship slammed into the outrigger, splintering it into a dozen jagged pieces. She felt herself being dragged along the vessel's side, her skin shredded by hundreds of razor-sharp barnacles.

A tyre passed over her head, just out of reach.

And another.

She could feel the churning of the propeller, feel its suction. She was going under. There was no way of stopping herself . . .

Then another wave struck, and the ship tipped towards her.

With a massive kick, she launched herself at the next tyre as it swung past. Her fingers closed on its rim. Instantly, she found herself being dragged through the water at high speed, her muscles screaming with the effort of holding on.

For a minute—maybe two—she was towed along. Then the ship began a long roll back onto its other side; and she was snatched up, dangling, into the air. As she struggled to swing her legs up into the tyre, she saw that Jik, too, had succeeded in grabbing one—but unlike her, was only holding on by one hand. He was surely about to lose his grip!

Somehow she managed to haul herself into a standing position. Now there were just a few feet of knotted rope above her, and the wooden rail that ran along the edge of the ship's deck.

But where was Jik?

She looked for him, but the driving spray hid everything. Praying that he'd managed to climb to safety, she pulled herself upwards.

The rope was slippery—half-rotten. It threatened to give way completely. But with a supreme effort she reached the rail and threw herself over.

As she did so, the ship tipped and the deck fell away beneath her.

For an instant she was airborne.

Then she hit the base of a stumpy mast.

She hit it at high speed, her body twisting violently around it, and she knew no more.

4

The One-Eyed Man

She was wrapped in something, swinging gently from side to side. The feeling was quite pleasant. It was like being a baby again. It was like being rocked in a cradle.

It helped her to ignore the pain.

She'd felt pain before—bad pain: an abscess under one of her teeth; that time she'd fallen off her bike and smashed both her knees. But she'd never felt pain in every bit of her body at once. She had to make a conscious effort not to howl out loud.

Where had the pain come from?

It was so difficult to think.

She could hear a voice—a woman's voice—speaking softly in a language she didn't understand. And there was a smell. Was somebody cooking food?

All the pain seemed to be flowing into her head now, thrusting up inside her skull until it felt as if it would explode. She groaned, raised a hand to her face.

There was a sudden noise; an exclamation. 'You wake up, Missy?' the voice asked urgently. 'You wake up now? Three days you been sleeping. Now you must wake up!'

'I don't want to wake up,' Hanna complained. 'It hurts too much.'

'I fix!' There was the sound of liquid being poured. A cup was placed against her mouth. 'Drink. You feel better.'

Hanna took a sip. The liquid was bitter, gritty. It was the most horrible thing she'd ever tasted. She pushed the cup away from her, but it was pressed back against her lips.

The voice was insistent. 'You must drink. This is good medicine. Fix your hurt real good.'

Hanna resisted for a moment longer, then swallowed. Somehow she managed to keep the disgusting mixture down. A sip of plain water followed. 'I think you are dead,' the voice went on. 'I think all your bones are broken, but praise be to Santo Nino they are not. I save you. The Maestro he say he does not want a white girl. He say a white girl is big trouble. But I say maybe you are a rich girl. Maybe there will be big reward. Are you rich girl, Missy?'

Slowly, painfully, Hanna forced her eyes open.

She was lying in a crude hammock made from an old fishing net. It was slung from the beams of an open-sided wooden shed. The shed was on a ship, she realized; and the ship was out at sea.

What was she doing on a ship? She struggled to remember.

A woman's face was thrust close to hers. It was a fat face—the skin stretched tight over a pair of bulging cheeks; the eyes almost invisible behind folds of flesh. A pair of glittering earrings, the sort you might wear to a posh party, dangled on either side of her neck. 'I ask you question!' the fat woman said urgently. 'Are you rich girl?'

'No,' Hanna just managed to say. 'I'm not rich.'

'But not poor, huh? You got parents. They pay money!'

'Money?'

Hanna closed her eyes again. Then opened them. The woman was still there. *What was she talking about? If only this brain-crippling pain would go away, maybe she could understand.*

A huge pot was bubbling on a stove nearby, steam rising. The woman shuffled over to it and began to stir it with a large stick. She was wearing a stained sarong, and a bright pink blouse, dark with sweat under the armpits. 'I am Nina,' she said. 'Called after the blessed Santo Nino. Your name is?'

'Hanna.'

'So how come you in the sea, Missy Hanna? You are in plane crash, maybe?'

A plane crash?

'No,' Hanna replied hesitantly. 'We were in a boat, a *dapang* . . .'

She stopped. It was as if a locked door inside her brain had suddenly been flung open and a blinding light shone through it. Instantly, agonizingly, everything came back to her: the typhoon; the shipwreck; the broken lifeline. *'My brother!'* she said frantically. *'I've got to find my brother!'*

She tried to get out of the hammock, but failed. There was something wrong with her left arm. She couldn't put any pressure on it. It must be sprained—dislocated or something. 'Please,' she begged. 'You've got to help me! Our boat got caught in the storm. My brother Ned got washed away. His lifeline broke.'

'We find boy.'

Relief flooded over Hanna. 'You *found* him! Where is he?'

'We find Bajau boy. Sea Gypsy.' Nina's bottom lip curled with distaste as she pronounced the words.

'That's Jik! He's our friend. There were three of us! What about Ned? Have you found him too?'

Nina stopped stirring, shook her head sadly. 'Find no more boy. We lose boy in the storm

34

also—Ramon. He was very good boy.' She paused, wiped away the sweat—or was it tears?—from her puffy eyes.

It was the medicine, maybe, but Hanna felt her pain begin to ease a little. Now she could think clearly again. They must radio for help immediately, turn the ship around. They'd need rescue boats. Spotter planes. Ned must be out there somewhere. He had his lifejacket. He was a good swimmer. The water was warm. He could stay afloat for hours and hours—days even—now the storm was gone . . .

She tried to tell Nina, but she snorted derisively. 'Where do you think this is? America? This is Philippines. Here we got no planes, no rescue boats. All the time people die. All the time they drown. It is God's will. If your mother is young, if she is strong, she make more brothers for you.'

'You're disgusting!' Hanna shouted at her. 'I want Ned back and I'm going to get him back!' She wrestled with her hammock. It tipped suddenly, sending her crashing onto the floor. She screamed in agony as she landed on her injured arm.

'You are stupid girl!' Nina scolded, helping her to her feet. 'You hurt yourself real bad!'

'I don't care! I want to know where the radio is! I want to send a message . . . '

But the fat woman was no longer paying attention to her. There was a sudden barrage of noise from the front of the ship—hoarse shouts, the shrilling of whistles. She glanced up the narrow gangway. 'Divers come back,' she said quickly. 'If the rice is not ready I am in big trouble!'

Nina shuffled swiftly across to the cooking pot, threw in some lumps of raw fish and a handful of chillies. Big splashes of her own sweat fell into the mixture as she did so, but she didn't seem to notice. 'Today they dive three time, not two time, so I must have food ready!'

'Is this a *dive ship*?' Hanna asked, confused. 'Are people on holiday?'

Nina gave a loud snort of laughter. 'No, they are not on holiday! No, sir!'

'But I don't understand.'

She prodded at the lumps of fish with her stick, trying to break them up. 'Soon you understand, Missy Hanna. Very soon!'

There were shouts from the front of the ship. Curses. The squeal of a winch. Peering apprehensively along the gangway, Hanna saw basket after basket of fish being swung on board by a crew of wiry, brown-skinned men. The fish were tipped onto the deck and rapidly sorted into large boxes. Ice was shovelled onto them, and they were lowered into the hold.

When the deck was finally clear, there were more whistle blasts. Immediately a crowd of small boys began to appear over the ship's side. There were at least forty of them—maybe more. None of them looked older than ten. Their heads were shaven, and they were wearing tattered swimming shorts. Each boy had a pair of cheap swimming goggles hung round his neck. Their skin was bleached and wrinkled from long exposure to salt water; their eyes red and swollen. Some of them were coughing; clearly sick.

They were silent. Completely silent.

Nobody spoke. Nobody smiled. As they hauled themselves over the rail they flopped down onto the slimy deck in utter exhaustion.

'Dive boys,' Nina said by way of explanation. 'Catch fish.'

'They catch them with their bare hands?'

The fat woman laughed explosively. 'No way! Frighten fish into nets. Bang bang bang!'

Still confused, Hanna was about to question her further when a furious high-pitched shout rose up from the sea below. *'Take your goddam hands off me, or Holy Moses I kill you!'*

It was Jik! It could be nobody else!

She raced to the rail and peered over. Drawn up against the ship's side were several small wooden boats, each one piled high with fishing nets. In one of them, Jik, wearing only a pair of swimming shorts, was struggling desperately with a muscular, shaven-headed man; kicking and punching with all his might.

There was no way he could win. A vicious, backhand blow sent him sprawling, and the man was on top of him in an instant, dragging him to the side of the lurching boat.

His shouts ended in an agonized gurgle as his head was forced under the water. Jik twisted and squirmed, but the man's immense strength pinned him down.

He was being deliberately drowned!

'Leave him alone!' Hanna screamed, not believing what she was seeing. *'Leave him alone, you pig!'*

Keeping his grip on Jik, the man glanced upwards at her. Her blood froze.

He had only one eye. The other was missing, gouged out of its socket, leaving a pink, fleshy hole.

She looked round desperately for something to throw at him—something that would make him stop before it was too late. There was an empty cooking pot near the stove. It wasn't very big, but it looked heavy. Using her good hand she pulled it to the rail and was about to pitch it over when Nina scuttled across and grabbed it. 'That my pot!' she shrieked. 'Gimme back my pot!'

There was a brief struggle which Nina won. 'But we've got to stop him!' Hanna yelled frantically, pointing downwards. 'That man's murdering Jik!'

Nina glanced over the side. She seemed more concerned about her pot than what was happening below. 'Not murdering,' she said matter-of-factly. 'Teach him a lesson. All boys need to learn lesson.'

As Jik's struggles began to weaken, the man jerked his head out of the water and thumped him hard on the back. He gasped loudly and coughed up a stream of seawater. Then he was slung over the man's shoulders and carried swiftly up to the main deck, where he was dumped, semi-conscious, in front of the dive boys. No words were spoken, but the implication was clear: 'Disobey me, and this is what will happen to you—or worse!'

Without pausing, the man spun on his heels and padded swiftly along the gangway to the kitchen. Nina tried to say something to him as he arrived, but he ignored her. He swung towards Hanna. She shrank away from him, but he grabbed her shirt. There was no escape.

'You call me pig!' he roared in a weird, cracked voice. 'Nobody call me pig!'

A sudden blow to her cheek sent her sprawling. She tasted blood in her mouth. She felt her legs begin to buckle . . .

He was about to hit her again when there was a shout from Nina. She was holding the cleaver she'd been using to cut the fish, waving it above her head. 'No!' she screamed. 'You're *loco*! You're mad! She is a white girl. If she is hurt they come looking for you. Police come. Army come. Ask many question. Many many question! You want that? Is that what you want?'

The man paused, then slowly released his grip. He shook his head as if trying to clear it. 'She insult me,' he said slowly, in a slurred voice. 'I don't like . . . '

'That's no reason for you to hit a defenceless girl!' Nina hurried back to the stove. 'You want rice? I got rice! It's ready. You like to taste?'

He grunted loudly, went over to the pot, scooped out a huge handful and stuffed it into his mouth. As he raised his head to eat, Hanna saw his face clearly for the first time. A jagged, badly-healed scar led from his forehead to his lower jaw, crossing the place where his eye had been. *Some-one—not so long ago—had sliced his face in half!*

5

Sharks Find Him

His name meant *'Master'*, she learned later, and up close he seemed strangely familiar. As Hanna nursed her throbbing cheek, she wondered if she'd ever met the terrifying Maestro before.

It was impossible of course—and she dismissed the thought. But scary though he was, she knew she had to risk infuriating him yet further. 'I've lost my brother,' she said desperately. 'He was washed away in the typhoon. Please turn the ship round so we can look for him! We're not rich, but there'll be a reward if you find him. There's bound to be . . . '

She broke off, anticipating further blows.

None came.

The Maestro stuffed a second handful of rice into his mouth, swallowed it with difficulty. He stared out over the stern. For an instant it seemed as if he might agree to her request.

Then he shook his head. 'He is dead,' he said gruffly.

41

'No he's not! He's got a life jacket! He's an amazing swimmer!'

'Three days in the sea, everybody is dead.'

'Not Ned! Not my brother. You don't know my brother . . . '

'Sharks find him.'

It wasn't an opinion, it was a statement of fact. There was nothing further to discuss. He turned away.

'Please!' Hanna implored, grabbing at his arm. 'Please help me!'

He shook her off angrily. *'Kaunan!'* he roared along the gangway. *'Kaunan peniap!* Rice is ready!'

There was a patter of bare feet and two of the dive boys appeared. They were older than they looked from a distance—maybe eleven or twelve— their bodies dwarfed by malnutrition, their bellies bulging. They stared at Hanna, wide-eyed, as if she was a creature from a different planet, before a bellow from the Maestro sent them scurrying to the rice pot, which they lifted off the stove with great difficulty. They struggled back to the main deck with it.

The Maestro started to follow them, but his way was blocked by Nina. She spoke to him urgently in a language Hanna didn't understand; but from the way they kept glancing at her, it was obvious that she was the subject of their discussion.

Eventually they seemed to reach some sort of decision and the Maestro stomped away.

Seconds later shouts and whistle blasts indicated that a new dive had begun.

'Sharks find him.'

It was only after he had finally gone, that the full meaning of what the Maestro had said hit Hanna. A terrifying vision of Ned's last agonized moments in the blood-drenched water sprang fully-formed into her tortured brain. She tried to push it away, but failed.

He *must* still be alive! The alternative was unthinkable!

'We can't just leave him!' she heard herself screaming. *'WE CAN'T JUST LEAVE HIM!'*

She was shaking now—shaking worse than her sick grandfather. She stared wildly at the sea. For one crazy moment she thought of jumping overboard and trying to find him. It was a stupid idea, she knew that—but at least she'd have tried. At least she'd have done *something*!

'Ned!' she howled. *'Where are you, Ned?'*

A large, firm arm wrapped itself round her. It was Nina. 'You must be brave,' she said softly. 'You must be brave girl. Santo Nino help you. I pray to him and he help you.'

Hanna turned on her accusingly. 'How? How can some stupid saint help me? The only person who can help me is the Maestro, and he won't do anything!'

'That is because he speaks the truth. Three days in the sea is too long. Your brother will not be found. It is time to mourn him, time to grieve for him. He is with the Lord.'

'No he's not! He's somewhere out there. I know he is!'

'As you wish. But I will pray for his salvation, as I pray for the salvation of Ramon, and all my boys who are lost.' Nina's voice hardened. 'And now, Missy Hanna, it is time for work.'

'Work?' Hanna struggled to understand. *'What work?'*

'You must cut the fish. I agree with the Maestro that you should do this. But I forget, you are hurt. Come!'

Before Hanna had time to object, Nina had spun her round and gripped her dislocated arm. Her strong fingers probed the injured joint. She gave it a sudden sharp twist. There was a loud click. Hanna screamed in agony—and then the pain disappeared.

'Up!' Nina ordered, raising her own arm. 'Now down!'

Hanna followed suit. It was like a miracle! Apart from a dull ache, her arm seemed to be completely cured. She stared at the podgy figure in front of her in awe. She was as good as any doctor!

'Now you cut the fish!' Nina waddled over to the gangway that led to the front of the ship and gave a loud shout. Seconds later one of the crewmen arrived. He was carrying a box full of small red fish. He shot Hanna a curious glance, put down the box, and disappeared the way he had come. Nina handed Hanna a sharp, thin-bladed knife, and took one for herself. 'Now you watch,' she said. 'And watch good!'

She fetched an empty bucket, squatted down next to it, took a fish from the box and expertly split it in half. With a swift flick of the fingers she hooked out its insides and dropped them into the bucket. Then she slit through the fish's gills, and removed those. There was a shallow wooden tub nearby. Next to it was a plastic sack of salt. She scooped out some salt and scattered it into the bottom of the tub. The gutted fish was spread out carefully onto it and covered with more salt. She repeated the process with a second fish, then a third. 'Now your turn,' she said.

'But I've got to search for Ned!'

Nina drew in a deep breath. 'Missy Hanna, you are nice girl, you are good girl, and you grieve for your brother, but that does not stop you from work. Here everybody work. *Everybody.* You see what

45

happen to your Sea Gypsy friend? You see what the Maestro do to him? The same thing happen to you if you do not work—only maybe even more bad. Now come! Take your knife and cut fish like I show you how!'

What followed were some of the most desperate, exhausting days of Hanna's life. Each morning she was faced with a mountain of fish to gut and salt. Then, when the fish had been salted for long enough, she was made to take them out of the tub, wash them in sea water and hang them up to dry in the sun on lines stretched between the foremast and the wheelhouse roof. Soon her hands were red and raw from the salt; scratched and bleeding from the needle-sharp spines on the fishes' fins.

The rest of the time she spent helping Nina to prepare the food, and fill and trim the battered kerosene lanterns that were the only form of illumination after dark. At night she slept in the fish-net hammock, slung from the cross-beams of the kitchen roof, while Nina snored on a mattress below. When the boys and men were on board, she was forbidden entirely to leave the kitchen.

She saw Jik most days, but always from a distance, so it was impossible to talk to him. He was diving regularly with the rest of the boys, and one

46

day she noticed that his head had been shaved like the others, making it impossible for her to pick him out individually in the water.

While she worked she thought constantly about Ned. Some days she imagined him rescued by some passing ship, safely back in port somewhere, waiting for Mum and Dad to arrive. But those were the good days. On bad days her terrible vision of his last moments returned, to occupy her mind entirely.

One thing was certain, though. She would never give up hope that he was alive.

Never!

Sometimes, when the boys were out diving, she was sent to clean their quarters—tier upon tier of crude wooden bunks with only a few sheets of thin plywood to protect them from the rain and wind. Here and there pictures were pinned up—tattered photographs of care-worn women who could only be their mothers. On calm nights, when everybody else was sleeping, she often heard the sound of sobs.

She asked Nina about the boys. They came from the poorest, remotest islands she was told. Some of them were orphans; others had been bought by the Maestro in exchange for money to pay off their parents' debts. *The Dreamboat* never went into port. Supply boats came—always at night—to bring food and fuel, and take away the fish for sale on the mainland. It was the only contact they had with the outside world.

'So the boys never see their parents?' Hanna asked, appalled.

Nina shook her head. 'Never. Stay here always. I am their mother now.'

'What about me and Jik?'

'You stay here too. The Maestro say, if he let you go, you will make big trouble for us.'

'But he can't keep us here!' Hanna exclaimed, horrified. 'We'll escape!'

'Nobody leaves *The Dreamboat*,' Nina said quietly. 'The Maestro does not allow.'

There was an edge to her voice—a note of menace that Hanna hadn't heard before. Despite the heat, she shivered. 'And what about you?' she asked. 'Is the Maestro holding you prisoner too?'

The fat woman roared with laughter, her eyes screwed into narrow slits. 'No, he does not hold me prisoner! The Maestro is my brother.'

6

Plans

Nina's warning had exactly the opposite effect on Hanna to the one intended. She became totally determined to escape. As she lay in her hammock that night, she racked her brains to come up with a plan that might work. She could think of only three possibilities.

One: she could get on board one of the supply ships that came to collect the fish, and hide away in it until it got back to port.

Two: she could swim to safety. She'd seen islands in the distance. She was a good swimmer, so maybe she could make it to one of them.

Three: she could steal one of the wooden dive boats. They were often left tied up in the water when the ship was anchored at a reef. They looked quite easy to row.

After a moment's thought she dismissed the first two ideas.

The supply ships were only alongside for the time it took to offload their deliveries and fill up with fish. They were always brightly lit, and never left unattended. Short of an invisibility cloak, there was no way of getting on board one of those unseen!

As for swimming, the Sulu Sea was full of vicious currents. She could easily end up being swept miles away from any island she aimed to reach. And the sharks would be waiting . . .

That just left the dive boats. It surely ought to be possible to climb down the ship's side and get away in one of them . . .

She must find Jik. Tell him her plan. He was a brilliant navigator and could steer by the stars. If they took turns at rowing, there was no reason why they couldn't make it back to Malaysian waters.

She knew where his bunk was—she'd seen his name scrawled above it when she was cleaning. It was positioned slightly apart from the others, next to one of the air vents from the engine room. With luck she'd be able to get to it without waking the Maestro, or the crew, who slept in cabins under the wheelhouse.

It was a calm night, the sea flat as a sheet of glass, all traces of the typhoon long gone. She strained her ears to pick up any sound that would indicate that somebody was awake, but she could hear nothing. Gingerly she swung her legs out of the hammock, stretching her toes as far as they would reach, before jumping lightly down onto the deck. Nina snorted, muttered something under her breath. But she was a heavy sleeper, and within moments she was snoring rhythmically again.

There was just enough moonlight for Hanna to see as she picked her way along the gangway to the main deck. She paused to peer over the rail. The dive boats were in the water, tied up at the ship's side. It should be no problem to get down into them, and away. Struggling to control her excitement, she edged past the sleeping dive boys. The hatch to the engine room was open, and there was a glimmer of light from below. She stopped, listened, but she could hear nothing. The crew had been working on the engine that day, banging at it with hammers. They must have left a lantern burning down there by mistake when they went to bed.

She could see Jik now. He was curled up on his bunk, not moving. It took her a moment or two to make sure it really *was* him—he looked so different with his shaven head. Then she tiptoed across and whispered into his ear. 'Jik, it's me, Hanna. Wake up!'

For a moment or two he didn't stir. Then his eyes flicked open. 'What you doing here?' he hissed fearfully.

51

'We've got to escape! We've got to get away from this horrible ship. We can steal one of the dive boats, but I need your help.'

Jik sat up, drew his knees into his chest. Fear and exhaustion were etched into his face. It was as if the brave, cheerful boy Hanna knew and loved, had disappeared, to be replaced by a frightened animal. He had a dark bruise on his cheek where somebody—the Maestro presumably—had hit him. 'Nobody leave this ship,' he said hopelessly. 'Anybody who try to escape they throw to goddam sharks. The dive boys tell me.'

'Then we must make sure we don't get caught! Let's go *now*, while everybody's asleep. The boats are tied up down there. I saw them.'

'Not dam possible.'

'Why not? We can be miles away before anybody wakes up!'

'The boats are locked.'

'Locked?'

'With big chain.'

Hanna's heart sank. 'You're sure of that?'

'Dam sure!'

'We can cut the chain! There must be tools down in the engine room. The hatch is op—'

A muscular arm snaked out of the darkness and locked itself round Hanna's neck. Unable to scream, unable to breathe, she was hauled upwards and backwards, and slammed against the wooden wall of the wheelhouse. 'I hear you!' the Maestro's voice bellowed into her ear. 'I hear what you say! I hear everything!'

Bare feet thumped down onto the deck beside them. There was a yell of pain from Jik.

The grip on Hanna's neck tightened further. She struggled, desperate for air. Darkness was closing in on her. She was losing consciousness . . .

She was flung onto the deck. Jik was thrown down beside her. He was moaning, a dribble of vomit seeping between his lips. Gasping for breath, Hanna peered up at the faces looking down at her.

It was the first time she'd seen the crewmen up close. They were small, brown-skinned men, their features eerily lit by the lanterns several of them were holding. Like the Maestro, they seemed strangely familiar . . .

Then she noticed something that made her blood run cold.

As the Maestro turned towards her again he rubbed his hands together. *One of them, she saw, had six fingers.*

Suddenly she knew for certain. Kaitan. A year earlier. A perfect holiday cut short by a vicious pirate raid that had almost destroyed her family. Their leader, the most brutal pirate of all, had six fingers. She clearly remembered Mum telling her.

These were the men responsible. *These* were the men who'd attacked Dad so brutally he'd almost bled to death; who'd robbed them of everything they had; who'd dragged Mum and Dad away, under orders to kill them and dump their bodies into the sea . . .

'Stand up!'

She was jerked violently to her feet. Jik was hauled up next to her. The terrified dive boys were dragged out of their bunks and herded onto the deck to watch what was going to happen next.

The Maestro made a quick gesture. One of the crew stepped forwards. He pulled rope from a bunch at his waist and lashed Jik's hands and feet together. Then he did the same to Hanna. She tried to resist, but it was hopeless.

They were going to be thrown to the sharks!

Whenever she'd heard of people being thrown overboard, Hanna had always imagined them able to swim freely, not trussed up like pigs. How long could she stay afloat without her legs and arms to help her, she wondered? Not long, she knew.

As she and Jik were dragged towards the ship's side she became aware of a noise behind her. It was the dive boys. They were crying, their faces wet with tears, their terrified wails rising and falling like the waves on the sea.

It seemed to take for ever to get to the rail. Jik was praying now, babbling something in a language she didn't understand, his voice almost drowned by the wailing of the boys. Hanna held her breath, anticipating the brief moment of free-fall before she hit the water.

At the rail her captors paused, waiting for the Maestro's command. *'Let it be quick,'* she heard herself saying. *'Please God let it be quick . . .'*

7

To Live or To Die?

'Throw them overboard!'

Hanna felt the men holding her stiffen. Then hesitate.

'Go on! Throw them!'

It took her a moment to realize that it was not the Maestro issuing the order, but Nina. She was waddling furiously towards her brother, clutching a lantern. 'Go ahead. Tell them to do it! But don't blame me if we don't have enough boys to catch fish! We got one dead in the typhoon and several more sick, and you want to throw these two to the sharks? Are you crazy? Are you out of your head? If we don't have enough boys we don't get even one single fish!'

The Maestro's single eye flashed dangerously. He indicated Hanna. 'She is girl, not boy.'

'OK. Let her dive too! She's as strong as a boy. Better she catch the fish, not feed them!'

There was a tense silence as the brother and sister confronted each other. They'd been speaking in English, Hanna realized, not Filipino. It was deliberate, she guessed, so the rest of the crew wouldn't understand what was being said.

The dive boys' wails built to a fresh crescendo. They were silenced by a shout from the Maestro. He strode swiftly across to where Hanna and Jik were being held. 'OK!' he spat. 'I spare you this time! But next time I don't wait for the sharks. I kill you with my own hands!' He drew a finger across his throat. 'Understand?'

The children nodded numbly. Their ties were cut, and Jik was thrown back onto his bunk. Hanna tried to catch his eye, but she was led quickly away by Nina.

The moment they were back in the kitchen, the fat woman erupted with fury. 'You stupid girl! Stupid, stupid girl! This is the last time I save you— the very last! Why do you not listen to me? Why do you not listen when I say to you nobody leaves this ship? Are you deaf? Do you not have any ears?'

'I'm sorry, Nina,' Hanna pleaded. *'I'm really sorry.'*

'What makes you think you are so special, huh? Is it because you have white skin? Do you say to yourself, these people have brown skin so they must be stupid? They have brown skin so they can be easily tricked?'

'No,' Hanna protested. 'I don't think that at all!'

'So why do you take us for fools then?'

'I don't! I don't!'

The tears that Hanna had held back for so long came quickly after that, flooding her eyes, blinding her, and there was nothing she could do to stop them. She felt tired, like death. How much more of this could she take?

She swayed, almost fell. She felt Nina's arms encircle her, pulling her into her ample bosom. 'You are foolish girl, Missy Hanna,' the fat woman said, her anger disappearing as quickly as it had come. 'But brave! For that I admire you. Now you must rest. Tomorrow you must dive, and that is a hard thing to do. Come, I help you to your bed.'

When Hanna was in her hammock, Nina pressed a quick, almost embarrassed kiss onto her forehead. 'Why are you being so nice to me?' Hanna asked, as she turned away.

Nina paused. A look of profound sadness crossed her face. 'One time I have daughter. She was like you, a beautiful girl, but so fierce, like a beautiful eagle! Her name was Yolanda. You make me think of her.' She broke off, her eyes moist.

'What happened to her?'

'She get sick. Die. I cannot afford doctor fee. After that, I say to myself, never must this happen again, I must learn to become doctor.'

Hanna was astonished. 'You went to *medical college*?'

Nina shook her head. 'I am a poor woman! In the islands there are many famous healers. I go to ask them. Now I know many things. Many, many things . . . '

'That's how you knew how to mend my arm?'

She nodded. 'Now you must sleep. Get strength for tomorrow. And no more escaping, OK?'

'OK.'

The fat woman shuffled across to her mattress and flopped down heavily. Within seconds she was snoring loudly.

Hanna closed her eyes, but sleep refused to come. She was lucky to be alive. She had no doubt that the Maestro and his crew had meant to throw her and Jik to their deaths. She was certain now that they were the pirates who'd kidnapped Mum and Dad. But what were they doing in this ancient fishing boat so far from home? They were from Tawi-Tawi, away to the south. Something very serious must have happened to make them come all this way.

Was it something to do with the terrible scar on the Maestro's face? she wondered. Had somebody tried to kill him for not carrying out the orders he'd been given on that terrible night a year ago—orders to murder Mum and Dad, and hide the evidence?

Only one person would want to take such revenge.

But he was dead.

Or was he?

Had the evil Datuk—the man responsible for everything that had happened—somehow survived? Was he even now planning more wicked schemes?

No, it was impossible! She dismissed the thought.

But as she lay awake, waiting for what the next day would bring, she could see his face, with its hard, cruel eyes and crocodile jaw as clearly as if he was standing in front of her . . .

8

Going Down

The grey light of early dawn. The shrill of a whistle. The bang-bang-bang of a stick on the boys' bunks to rouse them. Nina urging Hanna from her hammock, thrusting a cup of water into her hands.

Trembling from lack of sleep, she took a small sip.

'All!' Nina ordered. 'Drink all! If not you get sick in sea!'

Hanna did what she was told. She looked down at herself. She was still wearing the red shirt and grey shorts she'd put on so long ago back on Kaitan, and not taken off since. She'd have to swim in those, she supposed. If only she had the smooth, slinky, lycra costume Mum had given her for her birthday! She would be so much more comfortable in that.

A second whistle blast. A volley of loud shouts.

'Hurry!' Nina urged her, pushing her swiftly along the gangway to the main deck.

The dive boys were running ahead of her, pulling on their goggles as they went. She spotted

Jik, the bruise on his cheek livid in the early morning light. She gave him a smile, but it was not returned. She peered over the side. The crew were already in the dive boats, oars raised, ready to go. As she waited, uncertain, the Maestro strode over to her. He was half-dragging, half-carrying a small boy of eight or so.

'This Toto,' he said harshly. 'He speak English. He tell you what you do.' He handed her a pair of blue goggles, the straps frayed and split with long use. Hanna was still struggling with them when the order to dive came.

'Come!' She felt Toto's rough little hand in hers. He flashed her a quick smile and led her to the rail. It seemed a long way down to the water—further even than Dead Man's Leap—but Toto didn't hesitate. 'Jump!' he yelled.

Still holding his hand, Hanna threw herself into space.

It was like being in a mad bombing raid. Small brown bodies exploded into the water all around her. Then, suddenly, everybody was swimming as fast as they could, following the dive boats that had set off at high speed towards the nearby reef.

Hanna had taken part in lots of swimming races in her time—she had the certificates on her bedroom wall to prove it—but this was the wildest and scariest of them all. Several of the crew had stayed behind, only leaving *The Dreamboat* when all the boys were in the water. Their job was to urge on the stragglers. Hanna's goggles were letting in water, but when she paused momentarily to adjust them, a loud shout forced her to keep on swimming. The final person to leave the ship was the Maestro, powering past them with the speed and grace of an Olympic medallist.

It was an exquisite morning, the sun climbing swiftly above the rim of the ocean. Hanna's goggles were gripping better now, and with the growing light she could see clearly through the sparkling water. As she reached the coral, she peered downwards in awe.

It was the most beautiful reef she'd ever seen. It was like a garden—filled not with plants, but exquisite, fragile sculptures. Tiny blue fish darted between the branches of magnificent stag-horn corals. Huge fan-corals, so delicate they looked as if they would shatter with the merest touch, waved in the gentle current. Sponges and sea anemones pulsed and quivered as they fed on plankton brought in by the early morning tide.

There were fish everywhere. Parrot fish and angel fish flashing vivid blue and yellow in the sunlight. Shoals of silvery reef-fish, twisting and swirling as if taking part in some magical dance contest. And down at the bottom, tucked away beneath the overhanging coral ledges, were groupers and thick-lipped wrasse, guarding their territories as fiercely as any tomcat.

So many fish! But how on earth were they going to catch them?

Hanna soon found out.

The dive boats rapidly circled the reef, throwing out nets. Crewmen jumped overboard, tying the nets together to form a long funnel—wide at its entrance, narrowing to a bag-like shape at its end. They worked quickly and expertly, holding their breaths for incredible lengths of time as they wrestled with the billowing nets deep below the surface.

When they were done, one of the boats headed for the children, who were treading water on the far side of the reef, opposite the entrance to the net. '*Serosca* come,' Toto told her.

'*Serosca?*'

'Scarelines. To frighten fish. You wait, see.'

There was a sharp blast on the whistle and the boys immediately formed a line along the edge of the reef. The men in the boat handed out lengths of rope, onto which strips of white plastic had been tied. At one end of each rope was a bamboo handle; at the other end, a heavy lump of coral rock. The boys dropped the rocks onto the floor of the reef and gripped the floating handles. The plastic strips flared out in the current, forming a waving, swirling curtain that no fish would dare to cross. Urged on by Toto, Hanna followed suit, positioning her scareline next to his. 'We stay close,' Toto told her anxiously. 'If not, Maestro get serious mad!'

Hanna nodded; gripped her handle tightly. She felt tense—unsure of what to do next. The whistle shrilled again, and the boys plunged beneath the surface. Sucking in a huge breath, she followed them down.

It was only when she was under water that she understood exactly what was going on. Keeping close together, the boys began to swim slowly forwards using a sort of jerky doggy paddle, lifting and dropping their heavy rocks onto the reef below.

Thump! Thump! Thump! The noise was like the pounding of horses' hooves, as the line of jagged rocks smashed into the delicate coral. As their fragile hiding places collapsed around them, terrified fish shot forwards, desperate to save themselves, all the time being herded towards the waiting nets.

Hanna watched, stunned, until she was forced to rise to the surface for air. A reef as beautiful as this must have taken centuries to grow. It was now being destroyed in minutes for the sake of a few baskets of fish. There was no way she was going to take part in that! No way at all!

As she peered round desperately, Toto surfaced beside her, his small face distorted with fear. *'Do scareline!'* he screamed at her. *'Do scareline or the Maestro kill us!'*

'But it's destroying the coral!' Hanna protested.

'You want to die? Is that what you want? Please, Missy! Please do scareline!'

He was begging now, tears streaming from his eyes. He looked so young, so vulnerable.

She had no option.

She steeled herself, took a deep breath, and followed by a relieved Toto, plunged down to rejoin the boys.

It was desperately tiring, desperately distressing. Hanna forced herself onwards, her heavy rock pulverizing the reef beneath her. Exquisite fan corals exploded into a thousand tiny fragments. Sponges and sea anemones were ripped from their moorings and squashed to pulp. A large octopus, trapped by one of its tentacles beneath a fallen ledge of coral, died in a swirl of sepia ink.

On and on they went, rising now and then to gulp in a lungful of air, before plunging immediately down again to continue their destruction. More and more fish, forced out from their hiding places, darted forwards into the net, until it was a mass of writhing, flashing, silvery bodies.

Then, as suddenly as it had begun, the dive

was over. Crewmen were leaping into the water, closing the net as they went, trapping the encircled fish. It was a mammoth catch. It seemed impossible that any living creature on the reef could have escaped. All that was left behind was a wasteland of broken coral. If a bomb had exploded, the destruction could not have been more complete.

It seemed to take for ever to winch the baskets of fish up into the ship, and get them sorted and stowed. While the work was going on, Hanna and the boys were made to stay in the water. She spotted Jik, a little apart from the rest, clinging to the ship's rusty anchor chain, and swam across to him. It was the first time she'd seen him since the dive had begun. He looked pale and exhausted. 'I'm sorry about last night,' she began. 'I didn't mean . . . '

'Too dam late to be sorry!' he snapped, and turned away.

She felt too tired and distressed to say anything more.

There was food waiting when they were finally allowed up on deck. Hanna was forced to join the scrum as everybody jostled to grab handfuls of rice and fish from Nina's pot and wash them down with plastic bowls of sour-tasting water.

As soon as she had eaten, she slumped down next to the wheelhouse steps, desperate to ease her aching limbs. But there was no time to rest. Almost immediately the whistle shrilled for the start of a new dive, and Toto was scurrying across to her, hauling her to her feet, anxious that she should do nothing further to attract the Maestro's rage.

There were three dives that day, each one more destructive than the last; and three more the day after that. At night Hanna collapsed into her hammock and fell instantly into a deep, dreamless sleep that seemed to last only seconds before shouts and whistle-blasts roused her to start a fresh day. Eventually she stopped caring about the coral she was destroying. Survival was all that mattered—and making sure she got enough to eat in the desperate scramble for food between each dive.

As the days passed the diving got easier. Toto taught her how to hold her breath properly, to swim efficiently, and to conserve her strength. Whilst Jik stayed distant from her, locked inside himself, she found herself becoming more and more attached to the little dive boy. One day, when they were waiting in the water for the scarelines to be brought round, he told her his story.

He was an orphan, he said. He'd never known

his father. His mother—who'd taught him English—had been a teacher on a small island up near Mindanao. There had been a big storm, and the sea had come right over their island. His mother and his two sisters had been swept away, and he'd only saved himself by clinging to the roof of their hut. After that he'd been sent to live with his grandmother on Tawi-Tawi, but she was very poor, and there was not enough to eat. When the Maestro's men had come looking for dive boys, she'd sold him to them for two thousand pesos.

'Don't you hate your grandmother for doing that?' Hanna asked, horrified.

Toto shrugged. 'She is old. I eat too much. She have no choice.'

'And what about your mother and sisters? You must miss them?'

He looked wistful. 'For a long time I think, maybe they come back out of the sea. But now I don't think.'

Hanna felt tears prick at her eyes. 'They may come back! You mustn't ever give up hope!'

She was about to tell him about Ned. How she hoped that he, too, would one day return from the sea. But the whistle blew for the start of the dive; and when it was over, she didn't feel like talking at all.

About anything.

Her days became one long battle against fatigue. Sometimes, when she was diving, she actually fell asleep under water and shot spluttering to the surface, much to Toto's alarm. Now she understood where Jik's zip and energy had gone. It had been sucked out of him on the reefs, just as her own optimism and hope had been.

Unless they were rescued—unless there was some kind of miracle—it would be like this until the end of their lives, she realized.

They were slaves.

And they were being worked to death.

9

Too Many Ghosts

At last they could rest! After a particularly unpleasant dive, where the water had not just been murky, but full of tiny, stinging sea-fleas, the Maestro had announced that they would be heading to new fishing grounds, and there would be no diving the next day. For a while now catches had been getting smaller, until often there was only a single basket of fish at the end of a dive.

The reef had been picked clean. Destroyed utterly.

Hanna lay numbly in her hammock as the ancient ship rumbled northwards across the calm sunlit sea. As always, she was thinking about Ned. She could see his face so clearly when she closed her eyes. It was impossible to believe she'd never see him again. Mum must know they were missing by now—Jik's dad would have raised the alarm when they hadn't returned after several days. There was probably a frantic search going on at that very moment.

But the Sulu Sea was huge. It would be like

looking for a needle in a haystack. And anyway, they were now so far north nobody would ever think of searching for them up here.

If only there was some way of getting a message to them! There was a radio in the wheelhouse—she'd often heard the Maestro speaking into it when the supply ships came—but even if she'd known how to use it, there was always a member of the crew on watch up there, so she'd never be able to get near it. She even thought of putting a message in a bottle and throwing it overboard—except she didn't have a bottle—or a piece of paper, or a pen to write it with.

It was so frustrating! So upsetting! For this to happen after all the promises they'd made to Mum about not getting into trouble! She tried to imagine what she and Dad—and Jik's mum and dad—were going through right now. It must be horrible.

Eventually she lapsed into a shallow doze. She was dreaming about Ned—about the stupid things he said that made her laugh—when she was woken by loud shouts.

Alarmed, she tumbled from her hammock and hurried to the foredeck. She was just in time to see a huge black bird with a viciously hooked beak and a long forked tail diving in towards The Dreamboat at high speed.

It was a frigate bird—Hanna recognized it from wildlife programmes she'd seen back home. She had no idea they grew so big! Without slowing down it snatched a fish from one of the drying lines and soared skywards again, swallowing it whole as it did so.

A second bird followed.

And a third. There were others circling above the ship, gobbling like turkeys, waiting their turn to swoop in. Soon there'd be no fish left—and that would mean just rice to eat!

But Hanna was reckoning without the dive boys. It was their shouts she'd heard as they'd scrambled from their bunks. *'Lastik!'* they were yelling excitedly. *'Lastik! Lastik!'*

For a moment she was puzzled by what they meant, but then it became clear. They were clutching powerful-looking homemade catapults. There was a bucket of pebbles near the wheelhouse, and they quickly grabbed a handful each.

The boys were incredibly good shots. The next frigate bird got nowhere near the fish. A dozen pebbles slammed into it as it began its dive. One of its wings twisted back, broken, and it tumbled into the sea. Seconds later another bird joined it, struck down in a flurry of feathers.

Screaming with glee, the boys carried on firing, but the rest of the birds had got the message.

Gobbling furiously, they climbed quickly out of range and disappeared from sight.

Hanna peered over the side at the downed birds. One was obviously dead, but the other was still alive, flopping about in the water.

Not for long. Moments later a large fin broke the surface, and both birds were gone.

She was turning away from the rail, upset by what she'd just seen, when she heard loud applause. It was coming from the crew. The boys were being congratulated on their shooting skills. The Maestro, who'd been watching from the wheelhouse, came out onto the deck. For once he was smiling. He beckoned Toto over to him, patted him on the head and gave him a small silver coin from his pocket. The little boy beamed with pleasure as he took it, demonstrating excitedly how it was *his* shots that had brought down the birds. To the boys, the Maestro was a father, Hanna realized—violent and unpredictable, but still a father.

The only father any of them would ever have.

It was late afternoon when they finally dropped anchor. A range of mountains was just visible, rising above the sea to the north. It was the island of

Palawan, Nina told her. Hanna felt a very long way from home.

She looked around for signs of a reef.

At first she could see nothing. But then, towards the west, silhouetted by the rays of the setting sun, she spotted what looked like a cross sticking out of the water.

A *cross*?

Nina had spotted it too. She'd been behaving strangely all day—tense, irritable. Twice she'd gone up to the wheelhouse and Hanna had heard raised voices as she and the Maestro had argued about something. The sight of the cross seemed to make her even more upset.

When Hanna asked her what was the matter, she spat over the side into the sea. 'This is a bad place,' she said vehemently. 'We should not come here! I say to the Maestro he is crazy to come here. But he say there are big fish. Big, big fish. I tell him they are big because they eat dead people!'

Hanna shivered, despite the warmth of the evening. Whatever was she talking about? She sounded as crazy as her brother. *'What dead people?'*

'You see! You find out!'

Nina turned away; waddled swiftly to her bed. Pinned to the bulkhead above it was a garish picture of a saint. She knelt down heavily in front of

75

it. *'Señor Santo Nino,'* she began, *'source of all goodness. I kneel before your image. I implore your divine aid. Deliver us from the evil that surrounds us here . . . '*

There was a buzz of voices from the rest of the ship. The boys, who'd reluctantly put their catapults away, were now crowding the rail. The men from the crew had joined them.

They too were staring at the cross.

Except it was no longer a cross.

It was a masthead.

The tide was falling rapidly, and soon the outline of a ship began to appear. It was a warship, Hanna realized, encrusted with seaweed and barnacles, its heavily corroded guns still pointing skywards. It was completely upright, and as far as she could see, not damaged at all. It was as if it had just sailed there from some spooky underwater kingdom, and dropped anchor next to them. She almost expected to see barnacle-covered sailors waving to her from its deck.

Nina had stopped praying now, and rejoined her at the rail. 'Japanese ship,' she said unhappily. 'From World War Two.' She spread her hands widely. 'Many Japanese ship here. All sunk. Many dead body.'

Hanna stared at the surface of the sea around the stranded warship. It was alive with swirls and eddies. She could well believe that there were other wrecks just below the surface. 'Are we really going to dive here?' she asked, horrified.

Nina nodded. 'This reef is called *Tangis*—the Place where People Weep. Nobody come to fish here, only the Maestro. There are too many ghosts. I tell him he is crazy. I tell him we all die, but he does not listen. One time he was a good man. Now he is a crazy man—but what can I do?'

She turned away, slapping at her sides in frustration and anger.

Hanna followed her. She sensed an opportunity to quiz her. 'What happened to make the Maestro crazy?' she asked. 'Was it when his eye . . . ' She imitated the action of a knife.

Nina nodded. She scooped out rice from a sack, dropped it into the pot, added seawater from a bucket. It would soon be time for the evening meal. 'They beat him real bad. Break his head. Cut his face. There is much blood. They think he die, but I save him. Stitch him up. But his brain is hurt, and I cannot cure that.'

'How is his brain hurt?'

'He have much rage. Big, big rage. Only I can make him stop.' Nina sighed, glanced up at the wheelhouse, where the Maestro could be clearly seen, obsessively scanning the reef with binoculars.

'So who attacked him? Who made him crazy?'

Nina snorted angrily. 'Somebody who is even more crazy than him—big-time crazy!'

Hanna took a deep breath. Now was the chance to find out if her theory was right. 'Are you talking about the Datuk?' she ventured. 'Datuk Kamal?'

Nina slowly put down the bucket she was holding. 'How you know about him?' she demanded suspiciously.

Hanna hesitated. Nina clearly had no idea of her involvement in the dramatic events of the year before, and it seemed safest to keep it that way. 'I thought everybody knew about him. He was on TV.'

Nina seemed satisfied with the reply. 'They say he is dead. But if he is dead, why does he send men to kill us? Does he give orders from beyond the grave? I don't think so!'

'So where is he now?'

Nina shrugged. 'He has many powerful friends. If you got powerful friends it is easy to be invisible. Only when you are poor is it impossible.'

'So he could be anywhere in the world?'

Nina shook her head. 'I think he stay here, where his friends are.'

'Here?'

'In the Philippines. We hear stories . . . ' She broke off.

'What stories?' Hanna asked, her heart racing.

But the time for questions had passed. Nina was sniffing at the dried fish that was to be added to the rice, wrinkling up her nose. 'This mackerel stink bad,' she said. 'Maybe the birds should have eaten it. But today we don't catch any fresh. So what do I do?'

She shrugged, chopped it up and threw it into the pot.

Filling and lighting the kerosene lanterns was a job that Hanna usually hated. But that night she didn't notice the smell, or the greasy soot that always seemed to come off on her hands. Her mind was racing. So the evil Datuk *was* still alive! That radio call she'd seen him make as they'd left him stranded on Ghost Island a year ago had obviously got through. He and the Superintendent—his pig-like sidekick—must have been whisked to safety across the Philippine border before the Malaysian police—who'd been sent to arrest them—had arrived.

She shuddered. If the Datuk had had the Maestro's face cut for not carrying out his orders, what on earth would he do to her and Jik—who'd played a much bigger part in his downfall—if he ever laid hands on them?

It didn't bear thinking about!

And what exactly did Nina mean when she said she'd *heard stories* about him. What new crime was he involved in? There were so many unanswered questions. So many *worrying* questions . . .

As she lit the last of the lanterns and handed them over to the crew, Hanna vowed to find out the answers.

10

Dead Men Swimming

Hanna woke to the sound of raised voices. It was already late for a first dive, the sun climbing above the rim of the sea, splashing the wave-tips with gold. Nina was up, dousing her face with seawater from the bucket, the only form of personal hygiene she ever appeared to indulge in. Hanna asked her what was going on.

'The men don't want to dive. They say this is a bad place. The Maestro tell them if they do not dive they do not get money. He say they catch big fish here. Businessmen in Hong Kong, Singapore pay much money for these living fish.'

'The fish are going to be kept *alive*?'

Nina nodded. 'Put in tank. But the men say to the Maestro, these are not fish, these are dead men swimming.'

Spooked, Hanna glanced out across the reef. The tide, which was rising when she'd gone to sleep, had now fallen to its lowest point. The Japanese ship was completely clear of the water, straddling a massive ridge of coral. Far from being undamaged, it had no bottom, she saw. Surrounding it were angular shapes—obviously the twisted wreckage of other vessels. It looked more like a graveyard than a reef.

Praying that the men would somehow win their argument; that there would be no diving in this horrible place, Hanna lay back in her hammock and closed her eyes.

Seconds later they were wide open again as a huge roar went up from the main deck, followed by the sound of blows. One of the crew—a wild-looking, long-haired man called Nestor—burst down the gangway into the kitchen. He was bleeding from his mouth, spitting out teeth as he ran. He was closely pursued by the Maestro, who caught up with him near the cooking stove. There were more blows, the clatter of pots and pans.

Nestor collapsed, but was jerked to his feet, and propelled back along the gangway. As they went, the Maestro glanced back over his shoulder at Nina and Hanna. 'We dive!' he bellowed. 'We dive right now!'

They dived.

Nobody wanted to be in the water. The crew set off with extreme slowness towards the reef, their oars scarcely propelling the dive boats forwards. The boys, joined by Hanna, stayed close to the ship, not wanting to leave the safety of its familiar flanks.

As they waited, Toto swam up to Hanna. He'd taken to shaking hands with her formally before every dive, like a little old man. But that morning the handshake—and the toothy grin that went with it—were absent. 'Many ghost here,' he said fearfully. 'Japanese ghost. Boys say—'

She cut him short. 'The boys are talking rubbish. There are no such things as ghosts. Believe me!'

She would have said more to reassure him, but there was no time. There was a loud whistle blast. The Maestro, last to leave the ship, his disfigured face looking even more scary than usual, launched himself from the foredeck in a perfect curved dive, powering out towards the wrecks, urging the children to follow. Hanna pulled on her goggles, took a deep breath, and set off after him.

It was a strange feeling, swimming in a place where so many people had died. With each stroke Hanna half-expected a bony hand to reach up and grasp hers. Toto, not wanting to be left alone, stayed close beside her, his face pale with fear.

Weird as it looked from the surface, under water the reef was far stranger. The outlines of the sunken ships were clearly visible. All of them had holes blasted in their decks and sides—the thick steel peeled back like the open tops of sardine cans. When they'd first sunk they must have looked sharp-edged and alien in this submerged kingdom.

But not now.

Corals of every shape, size, and colour had anchored themselves to the corroding metalwork. Spiky black sea urchins and slug-like sea cucumbers crawled across what must once have been immaculate decks; angel fish and scorpion fish twirled in the early morning sun. The ships looked as if they'd been specially decorated for some fancy parade.

But the beauty was only skin-deep.

From every open hatchway, from every bomb-hole, faces peered out at them.

Big-eyed, thick-lipped faces.

Toto spotted the faces first, colliding painfully with Hanna in his efforts to get away from them. *They were human—they had to be—the faces of the long-dead sailors whose skeletons were surely still stacked in the sinister black interiors of the ships!*

But then Hanna took a closer look, and saw that they were fish—some of the biggest fish she'd ever seen. Massive groupers and wrasse; and, scariest of all, huge, sharp-toothed moray eels, looking like aliens from outer space.

They eyed the children evilly as they passed, as

if contemplating seizing them for a snack. Hanna had seen a programme about groupers on TV once. Some of them could live to be more than sixty years old, she remembered. As youngsters they could easily have fed on the decaying bodies of the dead Japanese sailors . . .

Was the Maestro seriously proposing that they should catch these monstrous fish?

He was.

Urged on by their boss's shouts and threats, the reluctant crew dived down to spread the nets. It took them a long time. There were swift currents, and the thin mesh frequently became hooked up on the jagged steel of the wrecks. But eventually the biggest of the sunken ships was completely encircled. Scarelines were distributed, and the whistle blew.

Hanna spotted Jik as she sucked in the rapid series of breaths she always took to oxygenate her blood before slipping beneath the surface. He looked as frightened as Toto, and refused to meet her eyes. She wanted to go to him, put an arm round him, tell him that he was still her best friend in the whole world; but she knew it was pointless. Would things *ever* be the same between them again?

Boom! Boom! Boom!

She was prepared for the destruction the

scarelines caused, but not the noise. As the rocks crashed down onto the steel plating of the ship, underwater echoes bounded and rebounded through its cavernous interior. It sounded like heavy guns firing.

Boom! Boom! Boom!

The small fish came out quickly, darting like quicksilver into the nets. But the big fish stayed stubbornly out of sight, preferring to hide rather than try to escape.

The children were ordered to swim back and make a second pass.

Boom! Boom! Boom!

This time half a dozen medium sized groupers and a single wrasse joined the smaller fish in the nets.

As she surfaced, Hanna saw that the crewmen were becoming agitated, wanting to abandon the dive. The Maestro ignored them. He made a sharp downwards gesture with his thumb. It was only when he was under water again that she understood what he meant.

Trailing a thin stream of bubbles, he swam swiftly towards an open hatchway, and disappeared into the dark interior of the wreck. If the fish wouldn't come out on their own, he was going inside to *force* them out!

Peering down through the crystal-clear water,

Hanna saw a large grouper emerge reluctantly through a bomb-hole—seemingly puzzled as to why it was being driven from its home.

A second grouper followed, then a huge wrasse. They swam in tight circles, avoiding the nets.

The Maestro reappeared, rose for air, then plunged down to the sunken ship once more. Hanna was so intent on watching him that she didn't notice what else had come out from the wreck.

It was pink and white, larger than a man's head, trailing a mass of rope-like tentacles. It propelled itself rapidly towards the wrasse and wrapped itself around it.

Instantly the huge fish was writhing in agony, fighting for its life.

A second creature, identical to the first, emerged. Its target was one of the groupers.

It tried to escape, twisting and turning inside the encircling nets, but in vain. A tentacle caught it. Then another.

Within seconds it was dead.

'Salabay!'

The crewmen had seen what was happening. Their shouts of terror were instantly taken up by the boys.

'Salabay! Salabay!'

Abandoning the dive boats, which were tied up

on the far side of the wreck, they turned as one, and swam frantically back towards *The Dreamboat.*

Toto dragged at Hanna, trying to pull her away as more and more of the sinister creatures emerged from their hiding places.

For a moment she struggled to understand. They were jellyfish. Jellyfish were common on the reefs. What was so different about these?

Then the sickening truth dawned.

These were box jellyfish, some of the deadliest creatures on earth! Dad had told her and Ned all about them the previous year when they'd found one dead on the beach at Kaitan. Unlike other jellyfish they didn't just drift, they hunted in packs, spotting their prey from immense distances, racing towards them at the speed of Olympic swimmers, injecting them with lethal venom from their tentacles.

Salabay must be their local name.

Urged on by Toto she swung round, desperate to escape.

But she'd forgotten about the encircling net.

It was slack, badly-set by the panicky crew. As she kicked out, her foot went through a hole that had been sliced in it by the sharp metal of the wreck. Instantly the fine nylon mesh closed around her ankle.

She was trapped!

She fought to get clear, but each kick seemed to make things worse. Toto tried to free her, but failed.

Then she saw the jellyfish.

It was bigger than the rest, swimming close to the surface. It had obviously sensed her distress and was propelling itself towards her with powerful thrusts.

There was no way she'd be able to get her foot free before it reached her! *'Go!'* she screamed at Toto. *'Just go! Save yourself!'*

He hesitated, but she pushed him violently away from her. He gave her a last despairing look, and headed back towards the ship.

Hanna turned to face almost certain death.

Each tentacle on a box jellyfish had four billion stings, she remembered Dad saying. The pain they produced was so intense most people died from shock, even before the venom had time to work.

Perhaps he'd got it wrong, she told herself . . . Perhaps it wasn't as bad as he'd said . . . Perhaps it was no worse than a stinging nettle . . .

She closed her eyes. Waited.

Then opened them again.

Something very strange had happened.

The jellyfish had come up close—very close. It was watching her intently, its clusters of tiny eyes glittering.

But it hadn't attacked!

She reached down gingerly, still trying to un-tangle herself. This time, to her immense relief, she succeeded. Without intending to, she moved her body towards the jellyfish.

It retreated.

She tried moving again, quicker this time.

Once more it shrank away.

It was afraid of her, she realized. Something about her was spooking it!

For a moment she was puzzled. Then the truth dawned: it was her red shirt. For some reason, it didn't like the colour!

Now was her chance! She began to swim cau-tiously back towards the ship.

She'd only gone a few yards when an agonized scream made her turn.

It was the Maestro! She'd forgotten all about him! He'd been under water all this time, and not realizing what was happening, had come up in the middle of the jellyfish.

One of them must have stung him as he sur-faced!

Nina had seen what was happening. She was at the rail of *The Dreamboat* screaming out her brother's name. In seconds, Hanna knew, the Maestro would be dead.

Unless . . .

She sucked in a deep breath and powered towards him.

It was like magic. As the jellyfish sighted her red shirt they shrank back, opening up a pathway of clear water.

A second sharp scream from the Maestro told her he'd been stung again, but she was closing in fast. When she reached him he was still conscious, but writhing in agony. She wrapped her arms around him, held him . . .

Would the jellyfish still stay clear? Would the magic of her red shirt still work?

It did!

An abandoned dive boat was floating nearby. If she could reach it, get the Maestro into it, they'd both be safe!

He was going into shock now, his body becoming rigid. Twice he slipped beneath the water, but Hanna wrestled him back to the surface. She tried the life-saving techniques she'd been taught in swimming, but he was too big. When she turned him on to his back, his body covered hers completely, hiding her red shirt.

Instantly the jellyfish moved in again . . .

She should leave him, she knew. Save herself. This man was her deadly enemy. He'd led the pirate attack that had almost destroyed her family the year before. He'd shown them no mercy then.

Why should she show *him* any mercy now?

She could be back in the safety of the ship in minutes. Nobody would blame her . . .

But she couldn't just abandon him! She just couldn't!

'Help!' she screamed. 'I need help!'

But all the dive boats were still out on the reef, and nobody was prepared to risk their lives in the water.

Or almost nobody!

A familiar figure had come to the rail. It was a small, wiry boy with a shaven head and bad skin. He was pulling on a shirt several sizes too big for him . . .

A red shirt.

Jik hit the water in an ungainly belly-flop, and swam rapidly towards her. Would the jellyfish be scared of *his* shirt too?

Hanna watched anxiously as he approached a large group of them, clustered near the net. They turned towards him, as if contemplating attack . . .

But lost their nerve and fell back . . .

Seconds later he reached her. Together they managed to drag the Maestro's stiffened body to the dive boat. With a huge effort they got him on board—the flimsy craft almost overturning in the process.

Jik scrambled in next to him. Hanna tried to climb in too, but her shirt got caught on a loose piece of planking and rode up under her armpits.

As she dropped back into the water to free herself, her skin was momentarily exposed.

A split second was all it took.

A pale white tentacle, speckled with poisonous blue, snaked out towards her . . .

11
Stung

It was a touch.

Just a touch.

But it felt as if a dagger had been thrust into her back.

It was the worst pain imaginable. Hanna screamed out in agony, and would have lost her grip on the side of the boat if Jik hadn't flung himself across and hauled her quickly on board. *'Holy Moses!'* he yelled, his eyes wide with panic. *'Holy Moses! You OK? Tell me you are dam OK!'*

The pain seemed to be getting worse, rather than better, but it was obviously nothing compared to what the Maestro must be suffering. An angry red welt was spreading across his naked chest. It looked as if he'd been burned by a blowtorch. 'I'm OK!' Hanna managed to gasp. 'At least I think I am . . . '

'Bring him here! Bring him here quick! I got medicine!'

It was Nina, waving her arms like a windmill from the side of the ship.

Jik grabbed an oar. Trying to ignore her pain, Hanna grabbed the other. 'Let's go!' she shouted.

It was like ploughing through a sea of pink bald heads. There were not just dozens of jellyfish now—there were *hundreds* of them, and more were arriving by the second. Back at the ship a rope was lowered, and the Maestro was winched on board. Hanna and Jik scrambled up after him. There was no known antidote to the venom, Hanna remembered Dad saying. It just depended how much had got into your bloodstream. And how tough you were.

The Maestro was tough. But was he tough enough?

He was unconscious now. Two of the crew bent to pick him up, to carry him through to the kitchen where Nina was waiting.

As they did so they recoiled in horror.

A severed tentacle, pulsing with poisonous energy, was still clamped to his waist!

Not daring to touch it, Hanna looked desperately round for something—*anything*—to lever it off him. There was an iron spike which the men used to break up the ice for the fish. She grabbed it, hurried back towards him.

But Nina had got there first. She was carrying a large bottle of brown liquid. She wrenched off the top, sloshed some of it onto the tentacle.

There was a strong smell of . . . *vinegar!* The tentacle contracted, twisted. Then, using her bare hands, she gingerly peeled it off, and flung it overboard.

Working quickly and efficiently, she poured more vinegar onto a thick cotton pad and bathed his wounds. 'It stop the poison working,' she explained.

'Is he going to get better?' Hanna asked anxiously.

Nina looked grim. 'Maybe. We must pray to Santo Nino. Now I put medicine onto him.'

She reached for a small pot, began to smear a thick brown paste onto her brother's skin.

'Hanna is stung too!'

It was Jik's voice, hoarse with anxiety.

Nina glanced up sharply at Hanna. 'He speak the truth?'

She nodded. 'It's not so bad . . . '

But it *was* bad. Up till now she'd managed to ignore the pain, but it was rapidly becoming impossible. It felt as if her whole back was on fire.

'Lie down!'

In an instant Hanna was flat on her stomach. Nina tutted with irritation as she examined the wound. 'Why do you not tell me of this before?'

Hanna tried to say something, but Nina wasn't

listening. There was a fresh reek of vinegar as the bottle was uncorked. Hanna screamed out as the acid bit into her lacerated skin.

For a minute the pain got worse.

Then, amazingly, it began to ease. She felt the soft press of Nina's fingers as she massaged in some of the brown paste she'd been applying to the Maestro. 'Now you OK!' she announced curtly, pulling down her shirt, and turning back to her brother.

Hanna got slowly to her feet. Her back was still painful, and would hurt her for many days to come, but the vinegar—and whatever nameless herbs and roots had been pounded to make the magic paste—had done the trick! The worst of the agony was gone. Once more she was amazed at Nina's skill.

Nina worked on the Maestro for a while longer. He was still unconscious, but his breathing was becoming easier. Eventually she stood up and gave orders for him to be carried to his cabin. Two of the crew hurried forward to obey her, taking him tenderly in their arms. Hanna was astonished by their concern. Surely they must hate the Maestro as much as she did for everything he'd put them through?

Yet it didn't seem so.

They laid him gently on his bunk and stepped

away. As they did so a sudden thought occurred to her. *'Toto?'* she asked. *'Where's Toto?'*

The men glanced at each other, alarmed. One of the dive boys, who'd been watching through the doorway, raced off to check Toto's bunk.

It was empty.

A buzz of worried conversation rose up from the boys.

'They say they don't know where he is,' Nina told Hanna. 'They thought he was with you.'

'He was! But I sent him back to the ship. He had plenty of time . . . '

Hanna rushed to the rail, peered down into the water. The jellyfish were still there, but there were fewer of them now.

Except in one place, mid-way between the ship and the reef.

There, they were gathered into a tight cluster, their tentacles wrapped round a floating object. Some sort of feeding frenzy seemed to be taking place, with more and more of them hurrying to join in.

As Hanna watched, a foot emerged above the water—a small, brown, pink-soled foot.

A child's foot.

'Toto!' she screamed. *'Toto!'*

* * *

They got Toto back eventually. The men had to collect the scattered dive boats first, then prise the writhing creatures from his body using boat-hooks. His skin was a bloody mess, criss-crossed with tentacle burns and what could only be bite-marks.

But it wasn't his injuries that Hanna found most distressing. It was his face. It was distorted into an expression of such appalling agony that the sight of it would stay seared into her brain for ever.

As they laid his tiny corpse on the deck, she finally cracked. 'I hate this ship,' she screamed at Nina and the crew. 'I hate it! Why does all this have to happen? Why? Just so greedy people like the Maestro—like all of you—can get money from catching fish! You don't care what you destroy to do it. Whether it's a beautiful coral reef, or this boy's life. We should never have come here! Never! Start the engines! Start them! I want to get away from here! A long, long way away!'

She turned, and raced down the gangway to the kitchen. She flung herself onto Nina's bed sobbing her heart out.

The engines did start up. Through her sobs she heard Nina's sharp voice issuing orders to the crew. The dive boats were winched on board, and the ancient ship began to gather speed.

As the sinister reef faded from view, she became aware of a small figure tiptoeing into the kitchen, dropping into a crouch beside her. Like her, he was wearing a red shirt.

He reached out, took her hand, and held it.

12
Deliverance

They buried Toto beneath a group of stunted casuarina trees on a small rocky island a day's journey westwards from the reef. He was wrapped in an old sarong. Hanna found some tiny, white, bell-shaped flowers trailing down the rocks, and made posies of them. As Nina recited prayers, the children stood together on the edge of the grave and threw the flowers onto the small, frail body. Hanna shed no tears. Unlike the dive boys, who wept freely, she had none left to give.

The Dreamboat was anchored offshore, and after they'd said their final goodbyes to Toto, they returned to it in the dive boats. As Hanna and Jik climbed back on board, Nina, who had gone on ahead, emerged from the Maestro's cabin. 'My brother wish to speak with you both,' she said urgently.

They followed her inside.

Though he'd regained consciousness the night before, it was the first time they'd seen the Maestro since the rescue, and they recoiled in shock. His skin was bright red, his entire body so badly swollen it looked as if he'd been inflated by an air pump. Nina picked up a bowl of water and started to bathe him, but he waved her away. 'Sit!' he said to the children, pointing at the floor. His cracked voice was almost inaudible.

They did what they were told.

'You save my life,' he said.

There was a long silence. Hanna could think of nothing to say to him in reply—nothing she *wanted* to say. In the end she said, limply, 'Yes.'

'Why do you do this thing?'

She shrugged. 'We couldn't just leave you.'

'Many people would leave me.'

'She is a brave girl,' Nina interjected. 'Brave like an eagle. The Sea Gypsy boy, he is brave too.'

The Maestro ignored his sister, his single blood-shot eye still fixed on Hanna. 'I owe you very much. More than I can ever pay. Is there something you wish from me in return?'

'Our freedom!' Hanna shot back fiercely. 'Just let us go!'

The Maestro glanced up at Nina. Then he nodded slowly. 'I will arrange this.'

Hanna and Jik looked at each other. 'When?' Hanna demanded, her heart racing. 'When will you arrange it?'

'Supply boat come tonight. I will tell the owner to take you with him.'

'Where to?'

'Puerto Princesa. It is the capital of Palawan Province. There are telephones. An airport.' He hesitated. 'But in return you must do something for me.'

'Haven't we done enough already?'

He nodded painfully. 'You have done very much. But I ask this not for myself, but for my sister, my men, my boys. Please do not speak of us to anybody on the mainland, or we will be in big danger.'

'Why *shouldn't* we tell people about you?' Hanna demanded, indignantly. 'You're evil! You kidnapped my parents! You nearly killed my dad! You should be in prison. Locked up for ever and ever!'

She hadn't meant to say it, and regretted it instantly. Jik was staring at her aghast.

The Maestro looked stunned. 'Is this true what you are saying to me? Are you the daughter of the European man and his Chinese wife?'

There was nothing more to lose now, so Hanna plunged wildly onwards. 'Yes I am! And I was there on Kaitan when you attacked them. My brother and I were hiding in the jungle. We saw everything. You're pirates! Vicious, murdering pirates!'

'We are not pirates. We are fishermen.'

It was Nina who spoke. It was hot in the cabin, and she was sweating profusely. Big dribbles ran down her cheeks like tears.

Hanna erupted. 'Fishermen don't kill people! They don't attack people with *parangs*!'

Nina shook her head. 'What happened to your father was an accident. He is a very strong man and he start to fight with the Maestro. Jon-Jon, who is my nephew, tried to stop him, but his *parang* slipped, and he cut your father on his arm. We did not wish to harm your parents.'

Hanna snorted with disbelief. 'That's rubbish and you know it! You people were paid to kill my mum and dad. And if they hadn't escaped you *would* have killed them!'

'Missy Hanna, listen to me! In the name of the blessed Santo Nino I swear to you we are telling the truth! We come from a small island close to Tawi-Tawi. It is a very poor place. We are fishermen all our lives. But the army come to fight the Muslim rebels, and they take all our boats. How can we catch fish with no boats? We have no food. Our families are starving. Then this man Ahmad, who is a servant of the Datuk, come to us. He say he will give us a boat, and much money, if we kidnap the European and his Chinese wife on Kaitan Island, and then kill them. What are we to do?'

'Report him to the police!'

'The police are our enemies! So we say to ourselves, to get the money we will do these things he asks, but we will not kill the European and his Chinese wife. We will take them to our island, and when it is safe we will let them go. We are not to know they will jump into the sea before we can do this. Please, you must believe us. You must forgive us for what we did! Many times I have asked Santo Nino for forgiveness. I have made many novenas . . .'

Nina stopped. Her chest was heaving. She was clearly very distressed. To Hanna's astonishment the Maestro stretched out a hand in a tender gesture and rested it on his sister's arm.

It was so difficult to reconcile what had happened that night on Kaitan with what they were saying—so very difficult. She would never forget Mum's scream, and the terrible, terrible blood on the beach.

But perhaps, when people were desperate, when they feared for their lives, they sometimes *did* do things they came to regret later . . .

All the same, she could never forgive them! Never!

'I forgive.'

Hanna turned, astonished. It was Jik who'd spoken, his first words since they'd come into the Maestro's cabin. 'But your village got burnt down

105

because of what they did!' she protested. 'You could have lost everything!'

'It is the Datuk who make this dam thing happen—not these Tawi-Tawi people! It is him we must not forgive!'

Jik was right, she realized. If Nina's story was true, they were *all* victims of the evil Datuk. Hanna swung back to the Maestro. 'Is he the reason why you don't want us to tell anybody about you and your ship? Is it the Datuk you're frightened of?'

He shook his head. He was tiring visibly, gasping for breath. 'I am not frightened of that man. All the time I am watching, listening. One day I shall find him. Then I shall kill him . . . '

He let out a violent grunt. A sudden change had come over him. A look of murderous fury spread across his disfigured face. He stared around wildly, as if he no longer recognized anybody. *'I kill him!'* he bellowed, lashing out with his hands, smashing his swollen fists against the wooden walls of the cabin. *'I kill him!'* He began to shudder violently, like somebody being given electric shocks. White foam oozed from the corners of his mouth.

Hanna and Jik shrank back, terrified.

'Get out!' Nina screamed at them. 'Get out quick!' She opened the cabin door, thrust them outside, and slammed it shut behind them.

The shouting went on for a long time. Everybody

on the ship stopped to listen to it. The boys cowered fearfully on their bunks.

Eventually it subsided, and there was silence.

The door opened, and Nina came out. She was drenched in sweat, visibly shaken. 'He sleeps,' she said. 'I give him medicine. Come!'

She led Hanna and Jik to the kitchen, where she poured fresh water into a cup and drank deeply. Then she slumped down onto her mattress, exhausted. 'Since they beat him, he is not like my brother,' she said in a strained voice. 'He is like . . . an animal. Perhaps it would be better if you had not saved him.'

Hanna shook her head firmly. 'You don't mean that! I'm sure something can be done for him. An operation . . . '

Nina gave a bitter laugh. 'For that he must go to Manila. Or London. Or New York. Where is the money for that? They beat him so badly. So very badly . . . ' Sobs racked her massive body.

Hanna sat down beside her, took her hand. 'Tell me how it happened,' she said gently. 'I need to know.'

Nina sucked in a deep breath. Nodded. 'OK. I tell you. Ahmad, the Datuk's man, give us only half the money he promise for the evil thing we do to your mother and father. But it is enough. With it, we buy this boat. The Maestro always dream of having a boat like this, which is why we call it *The Dreamboat*. We go to fish for tuna in deep water, but we catch nothing.'

'Why not?'

'There are no tuna left to catch. Japanese boats, Taiwanese boats—big, big boats—catch them all already. So we must fish on the reefs. We use *serosca*—scarelines. We know it is wrong. We know it kill the coral, but what are we to do? We catch no fish otherwise. With the money we make, we buy gifts for everybody on our island, and at Christmas-time we go home.'

'That was when the Datuk's men attacked you?'

Nina nodded. 'Everybody say to us that the Datuk is dead, so we think there is no danger. We are relaxing, drinking beer. The boys are playing. Then these men come in a fast boat. They come right up onto the beach. They have guns, big clubs.

'Our men are drunk, cannot fight well. The Maestro try to fight, but they beat him with clubs. They beat him so hard his head is broken. Then they take a knife, cut his face. After that, they go away. Three of our men are dead. Many others are hurt bad. But the Maestro, he is hurt worst of all.'

Hanna was horrified. 'You took him to hospital?'

Nina shook her head. 'There are no hospitals

on our island. I take my needle and stitch up his face, though I cannot save his broken eye. All the time I think he will die, but he does not. It is Christmas Day, so maybe God decide to make a miracle. Later he can walk and talk again.'

'What do you do after that?' Jik asked, wide-eyed.

'We are frightened. People talk. If the Datuk's men find out the Maestro is still alive, they will surely attack us again, kill many more people on our island. So we decide to go to sea and not to come home again. That way nobody will know the Maestro still lives. Nobody will know where he is.'

'Except the supply boats. They know,' Hanna pointed out.

'We pay them much money—nearly all the money that comes from selling the fish. For that, they keep their mouths shut.'

'But you can't go on like this! Not for *ever*!'

Nina shrugged. 'What else can we do? If the Maestro get better from his rage, then maybe we can go someplace else. But every day he get worse, a little bit worse.' She paused, looked up into Hanna's eyes. 'So that is why, when you leave this boat I beg you to say nothing about us to anybody.'

'But what are we going to tell people? They're

certain to ask where Jik and I have been all this time!'

Nina pointed at the island where Toto was buried. 'I will tell the supply boat owner to say he find you there. I will tell him to say the storm blow you onto the shore. I will tell him there is a reward, and it will be given to him.' She stood up with difficulty. 'And now I must cook rice. We all must eat, even if we do not catch fish. The supply boat will come when it is dark. May God bless you for listening to my story.'

13

Bought and Sold

Nina was obviously badly shaken—her old self-confidence gone. As she ladled the uncooked rice out of the almost-empty sack into the pot, she dropped the scoop, sending Hanna scurrying for a brush to gather up the precious grains. There was nothing to go with the rice. There were no vegetables left—and no fish had been caught for days. For the first time Hanna understood how vital it was for them to catch fish—whatever method they used. No fish, no food. It was as simple as that. Only people with full bellies could afford to worry about coral reefs.

After they had eaten, she lit the lamps and Jik took them round to the crew. While he was gone, she went to the rail and stared out across the glistening sea at the dim outline of the little island where Toto was buried. Nina had told her it was called *Pulau Bahagia*—which meant 'Happy Island'. They couldn't have chosen a better resting place for the innocent little boy, Hanna thought.

She, too, should have been happy. If everything

went well she'd be back with Mum and Dad within a couple of days.

But instead, she felt an aching sadness.

It was because of Ned, she knew.

And Toto.

But it was more than that. She'd miss *The Dreamboat*, she realized. Despite everything that had happened, the ancient, leaky ship had come to seem like home. She'd come to genuinely like— no, *love*—the fat, clever woman who, in a different world, might have been a top surgeon or doctor. She'd miss the little dive boys too—and the tough, wiry crewmen.

She'd even miss the Maestro. It was his injured brain that caused his terrifying rages, she now knew. Beneath it all he was a good man—a father to his men and boys. It was only poverty that had forced him to become a pirate, and put him into the clutches of the evil Datuk.

The Dreamboat couldn't wander the seas for ever! There had to be some way they could all go home again!

Unable to come up with an answer to their plight, Hanna climbed sadly into her hammock for the last time.

It was almost dawn before she heard the

engines of the approaching supply boat. Apart from a brief, restless doze, she hadn't slept at all, her mind a whirl of conflicting emotions and thoughts.

It was a big vessel—bigger than the small fishing boats that usually brought their supplies—and as the crew of *The Dreamboat* scrambled from their bunks to catch the mooring lines that were flung from it, a row broke out.

'What are they arguing about?' Hanna asked Jik, who'd slept on a blanket in a corner of the kitchen, and was now sitting up, rubbing his eyes.

He got up, went to the gangway, listened. 'Supply boat men ask how many fish we got. The crew say we don't catch any. Supply boat men get dam mad. They say they don't give us any supplies if we got no dam fish.'

'But they've *got* to give us supplies! There's hardly any food or water left!' Hanna exclaimed.

The two children ventured down the gangway to see what was happening. 'I know these dam men,' Jik whispered as they reached the main deck. 'They come one time before. They are called Sawa and AK. I think they are bad men.'

In the flickering lamplight the two men certainly *looked* bad. Sawa, the taller of the pair, had shoulder-length hair pulled back into a tight ponytail. His arms were heavily tattooed with pictures of sharp-fanged snakes. His companion was smaller, lighter-skinned. He too had tattoos, but this time of guns—AK47s with curved banana-shaped magazines. Like Sawa he had a *parang* slung from his waist.

The row was getting heated. For a short while it looked as if there might be a fight.

Then Nina arrived.

She gestured sharply at the crew, who fell silent, and planted herself squarely in front of the new-comers. She launched into a long, impassioned speech.

'What's she saying?' Hanna asked.

'She tell them all about us,' Jik explained, a note of anxiety creeping into his voice. 'She say your father will pay big dam reward—much more money than they can get for any dam fish—so they better give us the supplies.'

Sawa and AK looked at each other uncertainly. Their eyes seemed dull. They were either drugged or stupid, Hanna thought. Probably both.

Eventually they muttered something in reply.

'They ask how much reward your father pay if they bring you to Puerto Princesa,' Nina said.

Hanna began to panic. Dad was always going on about how broke they were; how they couldn't afford stuff. He was exaggerating, she knew—they must have *some* money. But how much? She blurted out the first figure that came into her head. 'A hundred pounds.'

'Pounds?' Nina sounded puzzled.

'Dollars,' Hanna corrected herself. 'A hundred dollars.'

Nina translated. The two men laughed.

'They say not enough.'

Hanna's panic grew. It was as if she and Jik were being sold off to pay for *The Dreamboat*'s supplies! 'Two hundred dollars,' she ventured.

'Not enough.'

'Three hundred.'

'Not enough.'

'So how much *is* enough?' Hanna asked desperately.

Sawa and AK glanced at each other again. Their faces were flushed with greed. This time it was AK who replied.

'He say a thousand dollars,' Nina said. '*Melikan* dollars.'

'But my father hasn't got that much money!'

'Please, tell them you pay!' Nina was beseeching now. 'I say to them your father is not a rich man, but they do not believe me. They say all white men are rich. They say your father can go to bank!'

'It's not that simple,' Hanna began. Then stopped. Nina's face was crumpling. '*OK. A thousand dollars!*'

115

A look of joy replaced the despair. Nina clasped Hanna's hands in hers. 'Thank you, Missy Hanna!' she exclaimed. 'You save us! You save us all! You are not just a brave girl, you are a good girl. You are like an angel from heaven!'

The unloading began immediately. Drums of diesel fuel and drinking water were swung on board, followed by bags of vegetables and rice. Finally, huge dripping blocks of ice wrapped in sacking were lowered straight into the hold where they were stacked on wooden racks.

Hanna watched the process numbly. What if Dad *didn't* have a thousand dollars? What would happen then? Would Sawa and AK hold them prisoner until he came up with the money? She couldn't imagine Dad agreeing to that. He was bound to do something stupid, something that might get him—or them—hurt!

The feeling that she and Jik had actually been bought by the two men increased the moment the unloading was complete. AK grabbed them roughly by their arms and frog-marched them to the side of the ship, where they were forced down a flimsy bamboo ladder onto the deck of the supply boat. Sawa and AK scrambled down after them. The engine was started and the mooring lines cast off. As they drew away, Hanna peered up at *The Dreamboat*. The crew and the boys were lining the rail. Nina was with them. She looked worried. She shouted something to AK who was hauling in the mooring lines, but he did not reply.

A new figure appeared at the rail. It was the Maestro, his swollen skin looking almost black in the dim light. Clutching at his sister for support, he raised a trembling hand.

Tears pricking at her eyes, Hanna raised hers in return.

The supply boat's engines were powerful, and within minutes the lights of *The Dreamboat* were fading from view. The children were led to the back of the boat and ordered to sit down. How long would it take to get to Puerto Princesa, Hanna wondered? She tried to ask, but was roughly told to shut up by AK, who had positioned himself in the doorway of the wheelhouse, where he was exchanging loud, stupid-sounding remarks with Sawa, who was steering.

Dawn began to break. As the light intensified, AK began to stare at the children. At first it was just the occasional glance in their direction—but soon his gaze became fixed.

Hanna shifted uncomfortably. 'What does he want?' she whispered to Jik.

'Maybe he think we are good to eat.'

'That's not funny!'

It wasn't.

After a while, AK left the wheelhouse and came up close. He peered at them, as if trying to make up his mind about something. He had a strong odour of rotting fish.

Eventually Hanna could stand it no longer. 'Why are you looking at us?' she snapped in English.

AK gave a loud, uncomprehending snort, and turned away. He went back to the wheelhouse and spoke urgently to Sawa.

'What's he saying?' Hanna asked.

Jik strained to hear. 'He say we are very famous dam children. He say he has seen us on TV. He say the Sea Wolf will pay much money for us.'

The Sea Wolf?

Hanna felt a sudden jolt of alarm.

Who was this Sea Wolf?

And why would he pay a lot of money for them?

Sawa shot the children a quick glance, as if to satisfy himself that what AK had just told him was correct. Then he picked up the radio, and spoke rapidly into it. AK kicked the wheelhouse door shut, cutting off the sound.

Sawa was on the radio for a long time. Up ahead, the jungle-covered mountains of Palawan slowly rose out of the sea. There was a town clustered around a broad bay at their base. Could it be Puerto Princesa?

If so, they were almost there!

Hanna was thinking about Mum and Dad— wondering what she would say to them, hoping desperately that Ned had been rescued—when Sawa finished his call.

He turned to AK with a triumphant look on his face. Stuck up a grease-blackened thumb.

Then he grabbed the wheel, swung the boat sharply round, and pointed the bows away from the town, away from the rising sun.

They were heading west—back into the wild Sulu Sea . . .

14

Special Delivery

'*Where are you taking us? Where are we going?*'

Hanna hammered furiously on the wheelhouse door as the town and the mountains were left behind. Sawa and AK ignored her, their backs firmly turned.

She wrenched at the handle, but the door had been bolted from the inside. All caution forgotten in her rage, she looked round for something to smash it open with.

She found a metal boat hook. Jik tried to stop her, but she thrust him away and swung it with all her strength.

The door was solidly made, but it couldn't stand up to Hanna's furious assault. One of its panels splintered. Then the frame. The door swung open on its buckled hinges. '*Turn this boat round!*' she screamed into the gap she'd created. '*Turn it round right now! I demand that you take us to Puerto Princesa . . .*'

Sawa twisted away from the wheel and lashed out with his bare foot. His heel caught her underneath her jaw and sent her sprawling onto the deck. He would have kicked her again if Jik hadn't thrown his body in front of hers. *'Berhenti!'* the Sea Gypsy boy yelled desperately. *'Please stop!'*

Sawa glared at him angrily for a moment, then turned away and issued a curt order to AK. Rope was brought from the wheelhouse, and their hands and feet were tightly bound. Dirty pieces of cloth were tied across their mouths as gags. Then they were hauled roughly round to the foredeck and thrown into the bows, where they could be clearly seen from the wheelhouse window.

After that they were ignored.

All day long they headed west, the boat's bows butting into a growing swell, drenching the children with spray. Somehow they managed to get themselves into a sitting position, which at least allowed them to breathe properly. Hanna's jaw swelled where Sawa's kick had landed, and her gag tightened painfully; but there was nothing she could do to ease the discomfort.

Towards the middle of the day AK brought them water. As he loosened her gag to allow her to drink, Hanna began to protest once again. Her words were cut short as the bottle was rammed sharply against her teeth.

It was almost sunset when they saw the island— the first land they'd seen all day. It lay dead ahead, emerging slowly from a low bank of cloud. It was about the same size as Kaitan, but there the resemblance ended.

It was one of the strangest islands Hanna had ever seen. It was as if an enormous knife had sliced off its central peak, leaving a sort of level tabletop edged by tall, rocky cliffs. On the tabletop were the remains of buildings, their ruined walls and gaping windows sharply silhouetted by the setting sun.

There were a lot of buildings, all of them roof-less, reminding Hanna eerily of pictures she'd seen of London during the wartime blitz. More were revealed, half-hidden by sprawling creepers, as they got nearer. Jik seemed as puzzled by the place as she was.

She glanced back at the wheelhouse. Sawa was once more talking into the radio. This time the conversation was brief. When it was over he picked up a pair of binoculars and stared at a spot on the eastern side of the island. Hanna followed his gaze. As she did so, she saw a boat emerge from what was apparently a solid wall of rock, and speed towards them.

It was a small inflatable craft, coloured black. In it were two men, also in black. They had bala-clava helmets pulled over their heads, leaving just their eyes visible.

They approached the supply boat at high speed, cutting the engine only at the last moment. One of them scrambled on board. He had an automatic rifle slung across his back.

He strode quickly across to the children, reached forward and ripped the gags from their mouths. 'Who are you? What do you want?' Hanna asked, terrified.

A blow to the side of her head was the only answer.

He took a set of photographs out of his pocket and flicked quickly through them, glancing at their faces as he did so. Apparently satisfied that he'd got the right children, he jerked them to their feet, hauled them across the deck, and dumped them roughly into the inflatable boat. He threw Sawa a tightly-rolled bundle of banknotes before jumping in next to them. His companion swung the craft rapidly away. Not a word had been spoken.

The island was at least a mile away, but the powerful boat reached it in a couple of minutes. Her heart pounding, Hanna watched the sheer cliffs race towards them. Just when it seemed they must crash into them, the helmsman twisted the boat violently to the left, and then to the right. A narrow gap appeared and they shot through into a small, semi-circular cove with a narrow rocky beach. A concrete slipway led down to the water. Behind it, obviously blasted out of the cliff face, was a wide cave. Drawn up inside it, completely invisible from the air or the sea, were two large inflatable boats—much bigger than the one the children were arriving in. They too were black.

The helmsman brought the boat expertly into the slipway and stopped the engine. His companion took a knife and cut the ropes binding the children's hands and feet. With a jerk of his thumb he indicated that they should get out.

Stumbling awkwardly as the circulation returned to their limbs, Hanna and Jik did as they were ordered. The man gripped their arms and led them swiftly towards a curtain of camouflage netting that hung down to the left of the boat cave. He pulled it aside to reveal the entrance to a tunnel.

It was enormous—big enough for a full-sized lorry to drive through. The children were hurried inside. The air was dank and musty, the ground damp underfoot. On either side of the entrance large chambers had been excavated out of the rock. They were filled with old motor tyres and other unidentifiable junk.

Their captor dragged them onwards, faster and faster, until they were almost running. Here and there ventilation shafts had been drilled into the roof, giving tantalizing glimpses of daylight far above. Then, without warning, the tunnel veered sharply to the right and their way was blocked by a massive steel gate. The man touched a keypad and it slid open.

Jik and Hanna were hustled through into what was obviously a guard-post. Two men, also wearing black, looked up from a bank of security monitors. Their eyes tracked the children as they were hurried past.

On the far side of the guard-post was a dimly-lit corridor. Several heavy steel doors led off it, all closed. They looked like prison doors, with small sliding hatches set into them. Their captor took out a bunch of keys, opened one of the doors and thrust them through. It was slammed shut and locked behind them.

The darkness was total. Not even the faintest glimmer of light penetrated the underground cell.

Hanna felt as if her limbs had been frozen. For a long time it was impossible to move. Eventually she plucked up courage and reached out in the blackness for Jik's hand. 'Come,' she whispered. If they could find a wall, they could follow it round and at least get some idea of how large their prison was.

They took one step—two steps—forward. Then

stopped, terrified. There was a noise. An animal-like shuffle, followed by a sharp grunt.

Something was sharing the darkness with them!

Jik tugged at Hanna's hand, trying to escape, but there was nowhere to go. Hanna desperately tried to make sense of what they had heard. It couldn't have been a rat—rats squeak, they don't grunt.

Was there a *pig* in the room?

She sniffed. There *was* a pig-like smell—heavy, unpleasant.

Then something hit her hard in the stomach.

She let out a cry of pain and toppled backwards, dragging Jik with her.

Instantly, the creature—the animal or whatever it was—was on top of her. An arm wrapped itself around her neck.

A human arm.

It wasn't Jik's.

Hanna clawed at it desperately.

There was a scream. The creature had a voice. *'I'll kill you!'* it yelled. *'I know karate. I can kill with my bare hands . . . '*

The voice was distorted with fear. But it was one that Hanna would recognize anywhere.

'Ned?' she said tentatively, her heart pounding, convinced that her brain was playing tricks on her. *'Is that you, Ned?'*

15
Together Again!

If he'd heard her, he gave no sign. Ned—if it *was* Ned—continued to fight, tightening his grip. *'Get away from me! I'll kill you if you don't leave me alone!'*

'Ned, it's us!' she gasped. 'This is Hanna! Jik's here too!'

'I don't believe you! Go away!'

He sounded confused, terrified. Surely he must recognize her voice? Then it occurred to her. He probably thought he was dreaming! In the darkness it must be impossible to know whether you were asleep or awake. It was like being blind—no, worse! If you were blind, at least everybody else around you could see . . .

Her mind was racing. What would a blind person do if they needed to recognize somebody? If they needed to be absolutely certain who somebody was?

With no vision they'd have to use their other senses. Smell. Touch . . .

Suddenly she knew what to do. She prised Ned's hands from her neck and raised them to her face.

127

For a moment his nails scrabbled painfully at her cheeks, but then his fingers began to relax, exploring her nose, her mouth, her chin.

The fingers hesitated, uncertain. Knowing what somebody *looked* like, Hanna realized, wasn't quite the same as knowing what they *felt* like. How could she convince him?

Then she remembered. One of her ears was bigger than the other. Not *much* bigger, but Ned had often teased her about it when they were younger. They'd even had a fight about it once.

She took his hands and placed them on the sides of her head. 'Remember Big Ears and Noddy? Remember when you used to call my ears that?' she said desperately. 'One big. One small. Feel them.'

There was a long moment of silence.

Then came Ned's voice—his little boy voice. 'It *is* you!'

'Of course it's us!' Jik said. 'You think we are dam ghost or something?'

'I don't know. I don't know anything any more . . . '

Sobs came. Great hoarse sobs. Hanna put her arms round her brother, raised him gently to his feet. She pulled Jik up too, and the three of them stood swaying in the blackness, wrapped in each other's arms.

After a while Ned led them to a bed. He seemed to know instinctively where it was. The children sat down on it, their bodies pressed together, taking new courage from their closeness. Hanna took her brother's hand, stroked it. 'I knew you were alive,' she said. 'I never once thought you were dead.'

'I knew you were alive too,' Ned replied in a quiet voice.

'What happened after you got swept away?' Jik asked.

Ned shrugged. 'Nothing much. I just floated about.'

'You just *floated about*? In the middle of a goddam typhoon?'

'What else could I do? There was no point trying to swim anywhere, so I just floated about in my life jacket. It was quite hard to do sometimes. Water kept getting in my mouth, and I kept getting turned upside down.'

'What about the sharks?' Hanna asked.

'What sharks?'

She hesitated. 'I thought . . . I imagined . . . you'd been attacked by sharks.'

'I didn't see any sharks.'

'Not one?'

'Not a single one.'

'So how did you get to this dam island?' Jik asked.

'When daylight came it was there, right in front of me. I was pleased to see it, but it was quite scary. There was no beach, just a load of cliffs and rocks—and the waves were really big. I thought I was going to get smashed to bits. But then a boat came and rescued me. The men asked me what my name was, and about you and Hanna, and took some pictures of me. Then they put me in this room and I've been here ever since.'

Hanna was aghast. 'You've been in this room? *In the dark?*'

'Yes.'

'But the storm was weeks ago!'

'I don't know how long ago it was,' Ned said quietly. 'Sometimes I think it never even happened. When it's dark all the time you end up not knowing anything. You don't know if it's day or night. You don't even know if you're alive or dead.'

He was shaking now, his teeth chattering audibly. Hanna felt an anger rise within her—a fury more intense than anything she had ever known before. 'It's *torture*!' she exploded. 'You can't keep people locked up in the dark! It's not allowed! It's not . . . '

She glanced wildly around, searching the blackness for the faintest light. There was none. 'Where's the door? I'm going to make them let us out!'

'It won't do any good,' Ned said hopelessly. 'I shouted for hours. I shouted until I lost my voice, but still nobody came.'

'But you must have food,' Jik said. 'If not you die!'

'They push it through the hatch in the door.'

'What about toilet?'

'There's a bucket. It smells really bad. You've got to be careful not to knock it over.'

'That's gross!' Hanna exclaimed.

'I guess we'll all have to share it now,' Ned said.

'That's even grosser! No way am I going to stay here in the dark with that smelly thing!'

Hanna stood up, groped her way round to the door. *'LET US OUT!'* she yelled at the top of her voice, banging on it as hard as she could.

There was no response.

She got Jik and Ned to join her, hoping their combined shouting and banging power would do the trick.

It didn't. With tears of frustration pricking at her eyes, she was eventually forced to admit defeat.

Ned led them back to the bed. 'What do we do now?' Jik asked quietly, when they were seated again.

'There's nothing we *can* do,' Ned said helplessly.

'Holy Moses, we could be here for ever! We

131

might never get out! We might never see our mums and dads again!'

Jik let out a strangled sob.

He was losing it, Hanna realized. Fighting back her own fear, she said, 'We must stay tough. We mustn't give in. That's why they've locked us up here—to make us give in!'

'We don't even know who *they* are,' Ned said bitterly.

'Oh yes we do!' Hanna retorted. 'And it's not a *they*, it's a *him*. It's somebody called the Sea Wolf. He paid a lot of money to have us brought here.'

'Why would he do that?' Ned asked.

Hanna racked her brains. 'I don't know,' she was eventually forced to admit.

There had to be a reason. A very good reason.

Ned supplied one. 'Do you think he's trying to find that pearl—the one we were looking for?'

'*The Moon Pearl?* But I don't understand.'

'This is Big Pig Island. This is the place where it's buried.'

Hanna gasped in astonishment. 'You're kidding!'

'I'm not! One day the guards left the hatch in the door open by mistake. I could hear them talking. They called this place *Babi Besar*. That's Big Pig Island in Malay.'

Hanna turned to Jik. 'But I thought we were the

132

only people in the whole world who knew about the Moon Pearl?'

'I think so too.'

'You're certain you've never told anybody else this secret?'

'Dead dam certain. My granny make me swear. Only I know how to find the exact place it is buried.'

'But you must have discussed it with Ned before we started on this trip.'

'We talk a bit,' Jik admitted sheepishly.

'You idiots!'

She could imagine the two boys getting more and more excited as they planned their expedition—their voices rising as they speculated how much the Moon Pearl was worth. And she could imagine Jik boasting loudly about how only *he* knew the secret of where it was hidden.

Somebody had obviously overheard them—a waiter from the restaurant on Kaitan maybe—and realized he could make a bit of cash by selling the information to a willing buyer.

Somebody like the mysterious Sea Wolf.

It must be infuriating to be on an island where you knew there was a fortune buried somewhere under your feet, and not be able to find it! But it must be even more infuriating to discover that the only person who knew exactly where it was buried was missing at sea after a storm. No wonder the Sea Wolf had let it be known that he would pay big money to anybody who could bring Jik in alive. And no wonder AK and Sawa had got so excited when they'd realized who they had on board their boat.

Everything added up.

Or *almost* everything.

What were those scary black boats for—the ones hidden in the cave next to the tunnel entrance?

And why were there security cameras and armed guards?

You don't need guards and boats to search for a pearl, however valuable it might be.

There was obviously something else happening on this weird island with its ruined buildings and underground tunnels.

Something even more sinister . . .

16

Into the Wolf's Den

The children sat on the bed for a long time—exactly how long, it was impossible to tell. Ned was right when he'd said that in the dark time ceased to exist. After putting up with a painfully full bladder for as long as she could, Hanna was eventually forced to use the toilet bucket. It was horrible—especially since she was aware that the boys could hear everything she did. Thankfully neither of them decided to make a joke about it. There was water in a plastic tub, which Ned said was for both washing and drinking. It was *very* unhygienic. It was bad enough with just one person in the room. With three of them, conditions would soon become intolerable.

They were just beginning to feel sleepy—wondering if there was room for them all to lie down on the bed at the same time, or whether they'd have to take turns—when they heard the sound of footsteps.

A key rattled in the lock, and the door swung open.

A light flicked on.

Hanna and Jik shrank back, trying to shade their eyes from the sudden glare. Ned, who'd been shut up in darkness for days, was groaning in agony.

'*Come!*' a rough voice said.

It was the same security guard who'd fetched them from the supply boat. This time he had two companions. The children were hauled to their feet and frog-marched out of the cell.

Stumbling in their efforts to keep up, they were led along a maze of underground corridors. Like the tunnel up from the beach, they'd been hacked out of solid rock. From time to time water dripped onto their heads as it filtered through from the ground above.

'Where are you taking us?' Hanna demanded.

There was no reply.

They came to a staircase. It was made from rusting metal, and clanked loudly as their feet landed on it. At the top was another corridor.

This one had doors leading off it—dozens of them. Most of them were shut, but some hung open. Through them the children glimpsed long-abandoned offices, complete with desks and filing cabinets. Ancient typewriters and telephones, draped with cobwebs and splattered with bat droppings, were still sitting on the desktops. A yellowing calendar on one of the walls read: August 6 1945.

This place—this weird, underground office block—had last been used more than sixty years ago!

The corridor broadened out into a series of larger, interlinked rooms. Some of these had been recently modernized, with tables and chairs set up around the walls. One of them was obviously used for eating, with collections of sauce bottles on the tabletops. In the room were a dozen or so tough-looking, brown-skinned men, playing cards and smoking strange-smelling cigarettes. They glanced up curiously as the children passed, but said nothing. Ned, Hanna saw, was tiring rapidly. He looked so pale and thin after his long imprisonment in the dark. Surely they must soon get to wherever they were being taken.

Another metal staircase, this time newly painted, led to an open-plan area that seemed to be some sort of control room. Banks of computer screens lined the walls. Two men, probably Chinese, were keying in data, talking rapidly to each other as they did so. If they noticed the children, they showed no signs of it.

Eventually they reached a polished wooden door. Fixed to it was a sign reading: *Sea Wolf Shipping Protection Agency*. Beneath it was a picture of a snarling wolf. One of the security men knocked sharply.

'Come!' a voice said.

The children were ushered into a spacious office. There was a large modern desk, bare except for an expensive-looking laptop computer and an intercom system. Behind it—obviously cut into the cliff face—was a long, narrow window giving a distant view of the sea.

A man was standing with his back to the door, peering intently at a pair of flat-screen monitors mounted on the wall. He was immaculately groomed, with sandy-coloured hair, and was wearing a smart, lightweight tropical suit. He dismissed the guards with a wave of his hand, and continued to stare at the screens. One of them was displaying sets of rapidly changing numbers. The other showed a map of South-East Asia covered with tiny blinking dots.

For a long time, the man didn't move. The children glanced at each other uncomfortably, not knowing what to do or say.

Then, as if reaching a decision, he suddenly spun on his heels, strode across to the intercom, and spoke abruptly into it in English. He was giving the go-ahead for something—some sort of patrol it sounded like.

After what seemed an age, he turned to the

138

children. 'Well,' he said, rubbing his hands together in a satisfied way, as if he'd just won a prize in a lottery. 'Here we all are at last!'

Now, for the first time, they could see the man's face. It was strangely stiff, almost mask-like. A pair of thin lips was contracted into what could have been a smile. 'Don't you recognize me?' he asked. His voice was deep, harsh, American-accented.

The children shook their heads numbly.

The man's smile broadened. 'You're certain about that? Why not take a closer look.'

He approached, and peered at them one by one, his face centimetres from theirs. There was something about his eyes, Hanna thought, her heart beginning to pound—something about their hard, dark stare . . .

'I'll give you a clue,' the man said. 'The last time we were all together I was standing up to my waist in water, and you were in the process of hijacking my speedboat. I was angry, I remember. *Very* angry.'

It couldn't be! It wasn't possible!

'You're the Datuk!' she gasped.

'Correction, I *was* the Datuk. But now I am Charles Wolf, alias the Sea Wolf. *C. Wolf,* get it? It's my initial. Even my best friends don't recognize me. As for my enemies . . . '

'You've had plastic surgery!' Ned exclaimed.

'I've had every kind of surgery known to man. I've had my jaw shortened, my nose straightened, my skin lightened. And all the time—all those hours I spent in pain and discomfort recovering from the surgeon's knife—I've thought about you kids. I've thought about how you were responsible for everything I was going through, everything I was suffering. And I've thought about what I was going to do to you when I finally caught up with you again.'

Jik glanced round wildly, looking to escape. 'Don't even think about it!' the Sea Wolf snarled. 'My security staff are instructed to shoot on sight. In fact you'd be dead already—all three of you, if it wasn't for a little bird.'

'What little bird?' Hanna just managed to ask.

'An electronic bird. I find it very useful. Let's listen to it sing.'

He crossed to the intercom, pressed it. To Hanna's horror, her own voice rang out—closely followed by Jik's in reply: *'But I thought we were the only people in the whole world who knew about the Moon Pearl?'*

'I think so too.'

'You're certain you've never told anybody else this secret?'

'Dead dam certain. My granny make me swear. Only I know how to find the exact place it is buried.'

'You bugged us!' Ned exclaimed furiously, as the *Sea Wolf* released the switch, cutting off the sound.

'I listened to every word you said, from the moment the three of you were reunited. It's why I kept you in the dark. I always find that if people are denied the use of their eyes, they use their voices instead.'

He crossed back to where the children stood. 'I found your discussion most interesting, but you got one thing wrong. I didn't bring you here because of a pearl. In fact I had no idea the Moon Pearl existed until you so kindly informed me about it.'

'Then why *did* you bring us here?' challenged Hanna.

'I thought I'd already made that clear. I brought you here to kill you—all three of you—one after the other. It's a treat I've been promising myself for the last twelve months. A wonderful, delicious treat! And the fact that everybody—including your own parents, who made a touching appeal on television for news about you—believes you're already dead, lost in the typhoon, makes it even nicer for me. Nobody will *ever* come looking for you!'

He broke off. He was smiling again, obviously enjoying the prospect of what was to come.

Hanna glanced at the boys. They were standing

close together, rigid and pale, betraying no emotion. She was surprised at how calm she felt too. It was as if she'd slipped through a portal into another dimension where nothing could touch her, nothing could harm her.

Then Ned spoke. His voice was accusatory. 'So why don't you just kill us then? If you want to do it so much, why are you waiting?'

'Because I want that pearl first. When I heard what you said about it, I thought it was just kids' talk. But to be certain, I checked with one of my contacts in the gem trade. To my surprise he knew about the Moon Pearl. He told me it was found inside a giant clam a century ago, but has not been seen for many years. Reputedly it's even bigger than the famous Pearl of Lao-Tzu which is currently in a New York bank vault, and which is estimated to be worth forty-two million dollars. That's serious money. So serious, I decided to postpone the pleasure of killing you all until after you've shown me exactly where it's hidden.'

'Why should we show you? We're going to die anyway!' Hanna exclaimed bitterly.

The Sea Wolf paused. The smile still lingered on his lips. 'Oh, I think you're going to show me, I really do! Particularly after I tell you about the form of execution I have chosen for you. It was invented in China many centuries ago. It's called

"Death From A Thousand Cuts". You've heard of it?'

The children shook their heads numbly.

'It's like . . . carving a Sunday roast. The executioner takes a sharp knife and cuts a wafer-thin slice of flesh from the condemned person. It's designed to cause maximum agony with minimum threat to life. Then, after a suitable pause, he carves another slice. And another. They say that in the hands of a skilled executioner a thousand slices can be removed before death finally occurs. The whole process can take days—weeks even . . . Of course there is an alternative.'

'We show you where the pearl is and you let us go?' Ned said desperately.

The Sea Wolf shook his head. 'Oh no! That would be too generous. I shall never let you go! But I *will* make you an offer. Lead me to the Moon Pearl and you'll get an instant—and painless—death. A bullet in the back of the head. Otherwise . . . ' He made the action of a knife slicing.

There was a moment of silence.

A long moment.

Then Jik's voice rang out: *'Holy Moses, I show you! I show you where that goddam pearl is!'*

17

A Good Place to Die

A set of steps led to the surface of the island from behind a reinforced steel door next to the Sea Wolf's office. Climbing them reminded Hanna, weirdly, of a procession in church. Jik was in the lead, followed by the Sea Wolf. She and Ned were next. Behind them were two guards, one clutching an assault rifle, the other carrying a spade and pickaxe. The Sea Wolf was holding a pistol, which he kept pressed into Jik's back.

There were fifty-two steps—Hanna counted them as she climbed. At the top was a metal trapdoor. The Sea Wolf pushed it open. Blinking in the intense sunlight, they emerged into the open air. The trapdoor, painted to look like a slab of fallen masonry, was swung shut behind them.

The children stared around them in awe. Weird as the island had looked from a distance, it was much stranger close up. It was like a small town. Cracked concrete streets, lined with ruined barrack-blocks, ran at right angles to each other. What

looked like shops—and even a cinema—stood roof-
less and crumbling, their blackened beams pointing skywards.

They'd come out onto what must have once
been a military parade ground. It was littered with
fallen masonry and twisted metal, pockmarked
with bomb craters. In one corner the rusting remains of a huge gun lay split into jagged sections
by a direct hit. Nearby was a flagpole, miraculously
still standing, the tattered shreds of a flag dangling limply from its top. 'Who built this place?'
Hanna asked.

'The Americans,' the Sea Wolf told her tersely.
'It was their Headquarters. The Japanese bombed
it flat after Pearl Harbor. Only the underground
section survived.' He swung towards Jik. 'OK, his-
tory lesson over. Where's the pearl?'

The Sea Gypsy boy didn't reply.

To Hanna's amazement, and to the obvious
amazement of everybody else, he suddenly stretched out his arms as far as they could go, and
turned a complete circle. He then turned a second
circle, and a third. His eyes were closed, and he
was gabbling rapidly in a strange, sing-song language.

'What on earth are you doing?' the Sea Wolf
hissed at him.

Jik continued to gabble and turn. Furious, the

Sea Wolf grabbed his arms and wrestled him to a halt. 'I asked you a question!'

Jik opened his eyes. 'I pray,' he said softly.

'There's no time for prayers!'

'Only if I pray will I know where the pearl is hidden.'

'I thought your grandmother told you?'

'She is magic woman. She is big *umboh*. She tell me there are many bad spirits here. Many *saitan*. They guard the Moon Pearl. She tell me I must pray to them in a special way, and they will speak to me and tell me exact dam place.'

'You're talking rubbish!' The Sea Wolf pressed his pistol hard against Jik's temple. 'You're lying to me!'

Jik didn't flinch. He took a deep breath. He was being amazingly brave, Hanna realized. 'OK. Shoot me!' he said. 'Go ahead, shoot me! That way nobody find dam pearl.'

The Sea Wolf hesitated. He seemed uncertain. He was highly superstitious, Hanna recalled, but did he *really* believe what Jik was telling him?

Incredibly, it seemed he did. He lowered his gun. 'OK,' he snapped. 'Pray if you must!'

Jik didn't move. 'I've prayed,' he said.

'So where is the pearl?'

'The *saitan* do not speak to me yet. First I must go to pray at all four corners of the island.

North, south, east, and west. Only then will they speak.'

'All four corners!' The Sea Wolf's voice rose to a shout. Surely Jik had gone too far this time! Hanna glanced at the guards. The man with the rifle had clicked off its safety catch, and was pointing it at her chest. He was waiting only for the order to fire.

After what seemed an age, the Sea Wolf reached a decision. To Hanna's intense relief, greed had overcome his doubts. 'OK,' he said harshly to Jik. 'We'll do what you want. But if this is a trick, you'll regret it!'

Doing what Jik wanted took a *very* long time. Progress was painfully slow as they threaded their way between the crumbling buildings, hacking at dense tangles of creepers and elephant grass. The sun beat down relentlessly, and they were soon drenched in sweat. Clouds of tiny flies buzzed and stung.

They went to the northern end of the island first. Perched on a steep cliff overlooking the sea was a ruined chapel; a wooden cross surprisingly still in position on the wrecked remains of its altar. They paused while Jik gabbled his prayers, before turning south, gingerly skirting a large unexploded bomb.

After praying at the southern tip, Jik led them to the east, and then finally towards the west.

Hanna watched him closely as he prayed. His voice rose and fell as he circled. Occasionally he let out loud grunts as if something—spirits presumably—had entered his body.

As they slowed to cross a deep drainage ditch on their trek westwards, she caught Ned's eye. A tiny smile was playing on his lips. Did he know something she didn't?

Then the penny dropped.

Jik had already told them *exactly* how he was going to find the pearl when they'd first set out on this crazy trip! *'You have to stand in a special place in the middle of the island,'* he'd said. *'The pearl is buried where the first ray of moonlight touches the ground.'*

He certainly hadn't mentioned searching for it in broad daylight—or anything about saying prayers!

She looked at Jik with admiration. By taking them to all four corners of the island he was not only buying time, he was getting a good look at the whole place. If they were going to escape—and that must be what he was planning—the more they knew about Big Pig Island the better.

They reached the western corner at last—a rocky headland stretching out towards the setting sun. To Hanna's surprise, several other islands were visible in the distance. On one of them a lighthouse flashed and winked. Big ships obviously came this way. Maybe they could somehow signal to one, she thought wildly—make it stop! She scoured the horizon, but to her disappointment it was empty.

There was a crumbling concrete gun platform on the tip of the headland. Jik scrambled onto it. The Sea Wolf followed, looking hot and angry, his expensive tropical suit creased and sweat-stained. 'OK, pray!' he snarled. 'But this time I want results!'

Jik went to the centre of the platform, faced the setting sun and raised his arms. After a moment's silence a gabbled prayer rang out and he began to turn. Round and round he went, faster and faster, until he was pirouetting almost as quickly as a ballet dancer. Then he suddenly let out a loud shout, and collapsed, flat on his face.

For a while he lay still—so still that Hanna began to wonder whether he was unconscious. But then, slowly, he rose to his feet again. His face was distorted, his eyes staring. He was grunting loudly. It was as if his entire body had been taken over by a wild beast.

He turned towards the Sea Wolf. '*Cheap,*' he said loudly in strange deep voice. '*Pearl. Cheap.*'

The Sea Wolf took a pace backwards. He was clearly badly rattled. 'It's not cheap!' he exclaimed. 'The pearl's expensive. *Very* expensive!'

Jik ignored him. *'Pearl. Cheap. Come.'*

With his arms stretched in front of him like a sleepwalker, and still making loud grunting noises, he climbed down from the gun platform and headed back towards the centre of the island. The others hurried after him.

He was aiming for an area immediately to the rear of the parade ground. They'd crossed it earlier, when they were going south. It was covered with dense vegetation, interlaced with numerous narrow paths. Hanna wondered who—or what—had made them.

Jik was following one of the paths, seemingly impervious to the thorny branches that whipped at his face. There was a strange musty smell that Hanna couldn't identify.

Then, without warning, he stopped dead. The Sea Wolf, who was following closely behind with his gun drawn, pushed past, cursing loudly.

A few yards away, scarcely visible in the tall grass, was a rusting vehicle, its wheels missing. Jik pointed at it. *'Cheap!'*

The Sea Wolf stared at it for a moment in puzzled silence. Then understanding dawned. 'It's a *jeep*, you moron, not a *cheap*! Are you trying to tell me this jeep is where the pearl is buried?'

Jik continued to point. *'Cheap. Dig!'*

The Sea Wolf turned to the guard who was

holding the pickaxe. His eyes were glittering with anticipation. 'You heard him,' he snapped. 'Dig!'

The guard strode forwards, swung the pickaxe high over his head, and brought it down with massive force onto the rusty vehicle.

There was a deafening clang and the bonnet flew off into the undergrowth.

He raised the pickaxe again, ready for the second blow.

It never landed.

Three enormous wild pigs exploded from beneath the wrecked jeep. They were followed by countless tiny, striped, squealing piglets.

Roaring with fury, the huge adult pigs hurled themselves at the intruders.

The guard with the pickaxe was caught first, his body thrown high into the air.

The second guard followed. He had no time to level his gun before he was crushed beneath their trampling feet.

Then it was the Sea Wolf's turn. He fired wildly at the furious animals with his pistol. There was a shriek of pain from one of the piglets, which only enraged the big pigs further. They swerved towards him, their razor-sharp tusks glinting in the evening light.

He fired a second shot, but it howled skywards. He turned and fled.

For an instant Hanna and Ned stood open-mouthed, rooted to the spot. But then Jik raced past them. 'Follow me!' he yelled.

He didn't have to tell them twice. Legs pounding, lungs straining, they sped after him.

Jik seemed to know where he was going. He headed towards the ruined buildings, dodging into the nearest one. It must have once been a barber's shop. There was a cracked mirror on the wall, with a faded advertisement for hair tonic stuck to it.

They were through the shop in an instant, racing across the parade ground, dodging bomb craters. They were aiming for a large building at the far end—the former cinema.

They were halfway to it when a sudden burst of gunfire rang out behind them, followed by squeals of agony from the pigs. The guard must have retrieved his rifle and was using it to deadly effect.

'Holy Moses, hurry!' yelled Jik.

The children still hadn't reached safety when there was a second burst of gunfire. This time *they* were the target!

Luckily the range was long, and the bullets whined harmlessly past them. Hanna glanced over her shoulder. The guards had obviously not been seriously injured by the pigs. They were racing across the parade ground, catching up fast.

The children reached the cinema. Though its

roof was open to the sky, most of its walls were still standing. Why was Jik so desperate to get to it, Hanna wondered, as they sped through its gaping doorway.

She soon found out. They scrambled over a mountain of wrecked seats, and into the projection room at the back. There, half-hidden by an ancient billboard was a large hole in the ground. Jik must have spotted it when they'd skirted the cinema earlier.

It looked like a well, but it wasn't. There was no rope, and no bucket. A ladder, bolted to its wall, led downwards into the blackness. Jik swung himself onto it.

'We don't know what's down there!' Hanna exclaimed, petrified.

'Who cares!' Ned pushed past her and followed Jik out of sight.

18

Buried Alive

Hanna hesitated a moment longer, then leapt onto the ladder, and half-climbing, half-sliding, plunged downwards.

The shaft was very deep. It had been dug as an escape route, she guessed—an underground exit from the cinema in case of attack. She could hear the boys calling to her from below, urging her to hurry.

A tunnel led off at right angles from the base of the shaft. As she reached the bottom, Ned grabbed her arm and jerked her into it.

He was just in time.

There was an angry shout from above, followed by a burst of gunfire. The guards had found the shaft and were aiming down into it. Bullets ricocheted off the rough rock walls. 'Let's go!' Ned yelled, as a shot whizzed past their ears.

The tunnel was narrow, its walls damp and crumbling. In several places there'd been rock falls, forcing the children to squeeze past on their hands and knees. Ned took the lead. After spending so long in his cell, he was used to the darkness he said. Jik was next, with Hanna at the back.

A short while later they heard a shout. The guards had reached the bottom of the shaft, and were now inside the tunnel. There was a distant gleam of torchlight. The children tried to go faster, but it was impossible. The floor was slippery and uneven, littered with fallen rocks. It would be very easy to trip and break a leg.

The tunnel sloped downwards for a while, then curved sharply to the left. Gasping for breath Hanna glanced back. The men were catching up fast, their torchlight getting brighter by the second. The moment they got a clear sight they'd open fire. In this narrow space there would be no escape from their bullets . . .

A sudden yelp of pain from Ned. He'd collided with something. It was a metal gate, no doubt designed to seal off the tunnel in case of emergency. It hung open on its hinges.

If they could shut it—bolt it—it might just give them enough time to escape.

The children heaved at it desperately, but it refused to budge.

The guards were closing in fast now. Soon they'd have the children in full view.

'*Together!*' Ned yelled frantically. '*Pull together! One, two, three!*'

They gave one, last, mighty heave.

The gate pitched forwards and crashed to the floor, narrowly missing the children who leapt back in alarm. It was followed by a sudden rumbling noise. The tunnel roof, no longer supported by the gate, was starting to cave in!

'Look out!' Hanna screamed, as lumps of rock began to cascade around them.

The rumble turned into a roar.

The children turned and fled for their lives as countless tons of rock thundered down behind them.

They made it—just! Coughing violently in the dust-filled air, their eyes streaming, they peered back the way they'd come. The light from the guards' torches had disappeared. Had the two men been crushed by the falling rocks?

It was impossible to tell—but it didn't matter. The tunnel was blocked solid.

They were safe—at least for now.

It took a long time for the dust to settle. The children slumped against the rocky tunnel walls, burying their faces in their T-shirts to filter out the worst of it. They were numb with exhaustion, and acutely thirsty.

But they'd done it! Against all the odds, they'd managed to escape from the evil Sea Wolf and his murderous guards. And it was all thanks to Jik, and his incredible bravery!

'Were those *real* prayers you were saying up there on the island?' Hanna asked admiringly, when the dust had cleared sufficiently for them to speak.

Jik chuckled into the darkness. 'No way! I just say the names of all my brothers and sisters and uncles and aunts and cousins over and over again, very dam quick! It sound like praying but I am saying dam silly rubbish!'

'The Sea Wolf believed it.'

'He is dam silly rubbish too!'

They all laughed at that.

'What about those pigs?' Ned put in. 'How on earth did you know they were under that jeep?'

'Since I am little boy I go with my father to hunt pigs. They are very dam tasty to eat. He teach me how to look for their foots.'

'You mean footprints?' Hanna asked.

'Same dam thing! When I see them I know mother pigs and baby pigs make their house there. Mother pigs with babies are totally dam dangerous!'

'You're a genius,' Ned said. 'An utter genius!'

'That is goddam truth,' Jik agreed modestly.

They forced themselves back to their feet again. They must get out of the tunnel as soon as possible. There could easily be more roof falls, and they could end up fatally trapped.

They set off once more, with Ned in the lead, carefully picking their way along the slippery floor. The tunnel seemed to go on for ever, curving sharply from time to time. Their thirst was becoming unbearable. If only there was something to drink!

They heard the spring long before they got to it—a tinkling, trickling sound—but it was Ned who actually found it, his feet splashing into a large puddle on the tunnel floor.

Groping with their hands, they traced the water back to its source. It was coming from a crack in the tunnel wall. They tasted it cautiously. It was cool and clear.

They drank deeply, then washed off as much dust from themselves as possible. It was a wonderful feeling getting clean again! If only they had a bottle to collect some water in for later. For the first time in her life Hanna wished she was a camel with a big empty hump!

Soon after that the tunnel broadened out.

Hanna stopped. Could she feel a breeze on her cheek? Was she imagining it? And what was that smell?

For a moment she was puzzled. But then she knew what it reminded her of.

A filling station.

It was petrol!

The boys could smell it too. 'Hear noise also,' Jik announced.

Ned and Hanna strained their ears to hear.

Jik was right. There *was* a noise—a faint but insistent hum. It sounded like machinery.

Were their worst fears about to come true?

Was the tunnel leading them straight back into the Sea Wolf's evil clutches?

19
Trapped!

There was no alternative—they had to go onwards. The children crept cautiously through the darkness. It was vital they did nothing to give themselves away.

The engine noise got louder. It was no longer a hum but a constant, unvarying roar. What on earth could be making it? After a while Ned stopped. 'I can see something,' he hissed.

Hanna and Jik pressed up beside him, peering into the gloom.

A faint light gleamed up ahead. It was just bright enough for them to make out a large stack of what looked like fuel drums. That must be where the smell was coming from.

They edged closer. The fumes were stronger now, making their eyes water, and their heads ache.

It *was* fuel—diesel, and high-octane petrol. The drums were stacked on pallets, filling up the whole tunnel.

For one horrible moment it looked as if there

was no way past. But then Ned spotted a gap between one of the pallets and the wall. Was there enough space to squeeze through?

They might just manage it, Hanna thought as she peered cautiously into it. But what was on the other side? It was impossible to tell. They'd just have to risk it—pray that no one would spot them.

Jik volunteered to go first. He understood Malay, he explained. If there were people about, he could listen to what they were saying, find out what was going on. He'd stay hidden until he was sure it was safe, then signal to Hanna and Ned to join him.

'How are you going to do that?' Hanna asked.

He grinned. 'No dam problem!' He produced a length of fishing line from his pocket, gave her one end to hold, and took the other. 'I pull three dam times, then you come!'

Trailing the line behind him, he slid round the drums and disappeared.

Long minutes passed. The two children were starting to wonder whether something serious had happened, when Hanna suddenly felt the line jerk in her fingers.

Once . . . Twice . . .

Three times.

'It's Jik!' she whispered excitedly. 'Let's go!'

With Ned following, she squeezed herself into the gap.

It was a very tight fit. She was bigger than the boys, and several times got painfully stuck. 'Breathe out,' her brother told her. 'It makes your body smaller.'

It worked. Slowly, agonizingly, she forced herself through.

Jik was hiding in the shadows as they emerged. He slipped across to meet them, winding in the line as he did so.

They stared around apprehensively. They were at the rear of a large underground space that was obviously being used as a workshop. Chain hoists were slung from the roof. There were benches stacked with machine tools. On one of them, a powerful outboard motor lay half dismantled. In the centre of the workshop was a steel box, the size of a small shipping container. The noise they'd heard was coming from it. Numerous pipes and cables snaked away from its base.

'It's a generator,' Ned whispered to Hanna. 'For making electricity. We learnt about them in Science.'

'Very goddam powerful generator,' Jik put in. 'I hear the men say so.'

'What men?' Hanna asked apprehensively.

'There are two men here when I arrive. That's

why I wait so long before I signal to you. They are mending the engine, but now they go away. They talk about us. They say we get buried alive. They say the Sea Wolf is very dam mad.'

Hanna's heart leapt. So the guards who'd been chasing them hadn't been crushed by the falling roof. Instead, they'd assumed it was her, Ned, and Jik who'd been killed! She could imagine the Sea Wolf's fury when they told him what had happened. Not only had he failed to get his hands on the Moon Pearl, he'd been cheated out of the revenge he'd been planning for so long.

It was the best news ever! It meant that nobody was looking for them now. If they were clever—and careful—there was a real chance they could get away.

But first, they must escape from this underground warren!

At the far end of the workshop was a pair of large double doors. They hurried across to them.

Ned tugged at the handle. They slid open smoothly.

The children were met by a gust of fresh air—the outside world at last!

But where were they?

They peered cautiously out. Night had fallen, and the area in front of them was unlit. It was impossible to see anything.

Then the moon drifted clear of a cloud that had been hiding it.

'We're in the boat cave!' Hanna whispered excitedly. 'We're in that place we saw when we first arrived, where those big black boats are kept!'

The two huge inflatable craft were drawn up in front of them, looking like beached whales, their massive engines gleaming in the moonlight. Parked next to them was a tractor. Beyond them the children could see the slipway, and the cove.

'Look!' Jik pointed excitedly out at its gleaming waters.

Moored close to the shore was the small boat that had brought them to Big Pig Island. It was the answer to all their prayers! It was fast and power-ful. If they could get to it without being seen and start the engine, they could be miles away before the alarm was raised.

'Wicked!' Ned exclaimed under his breath. The boys were about to race out to it, when Hanna grabbed them and hauled them back.

Something had caught her eye.

A small red light was winking in the darkness. It was coming from a security camera fixed to the lip of the cave. A second camera was set up on the far side of the opening. They were night-vision cameras, Hanna guessed, no doubt activated by an invisible beam. Fortunately they were aimed outwards—the Sea Wolf clearly didn't expect intruders from inside the cave.

The children looked at each other in dismay. If they tried to leave, the cameras would spot them for sure.

They were trapped!

They were silent for a moment or two, trying to come up with a solution to their dilemma.

Then Ned's eyes lit up. 'All this security stuff,' he whispered. 'How does it work?'

'I don't know,' Hanna replied, mystified by his question.

'It works with electricity. No electricity, no security!' He indicated the generator in the workshop behind them. 'That's where the electricity comes from, so why don't we just turn it off?'

Hanna stared at him open-mouthed. 'Are you serious?'

'Dead serious! There's bound to be a switch somewhere. Then, while everybody's groping about in the dark and the cameras aren't working, we run like hell to the boat, get in and escape. By the time they get the lights back on we'll be long gone!'

'Now it is *you* who are goddam genius,' Jik said admiringly.

There was no time to lose. The repair men might be back at any moment. The children ducked back into the workshop and raced to the generator. After a few moment's frantic search they located a control panel. On it were rows of dials and switches. They peered at them closely, reading out the labels: *Air Breaker Indicator; Power Output Indicator; Loading Switch* . . .

None of them made any sense.

Then they found one that did: a large red button marked *Shut Down.*

'That means *off*!' Ned exclaimed, and promptly jammed his thumb hard onto it.

The effect was immediate. The roar of the engine turned into an agonized screech. Exhaust smoke belched out through its cowling.

Then silence.

The lights in the workshop flickered and went out.

'Let's go!' yelled Ned.

They charged through the double doors, through the boat cave and out onto the slipway. 'You drive!' Ned shouted to Hanna as they flung themselves on board the boat.

She scrambled into the driver's seat. She'd driven a speedboat before, so she knew where the controls were. She groped for the starter key. It should be on the steering column she told herself, like in a car.

It wasn't there.

Her horrified eyes met the boys'. 'I can't start this thing. There's no key!'

'You're sure?' Ned gasped.

'Dead sure! I've found the slot where it goes, but somebody must have taken it.'

'What do we do now?'

'I don't know!'

She peered wildly round. The slipway was in darkness, still deserted—but for how much longer? She could already hear raised voices in the distance.

She was cursing herself. The Sea Wolf's men weren't idiots. Of course they wouldn't leave a boat moored with its key still in it! Now they were stranded out in the open, with nowhere to go.

The shouts were getting louder. Torchlight gleamed.

Jik's voice: 'Come quick!'

He leapt back onto the shore. Hanna and Ned dashed after him. Where on earth was he going? Not back into the workshop, surely?

He wasn't. He was heading up the beach towards the two big black inflatable boats. He scrambled into the nearest one. Hanna and Ned followed.

There was a locker in its bows, with a hinged lid. He must have spotted it when he'd raced past moments earlier. He jerked it open.

It was empty, except for a coil of rope.

'Get in!' he said frantically.

'But we can't all fit in there!' Hanna protested.

'We'll hide in the next one. Come on, Ned!'

The two boys leapt into the neighbouring boat, wrenched its locker open, and squeezed inside. As they did so, lights began to flicker on. A back-up generator must have kicked in. Hanna just had time to see the boys' lid pulled firmly shut on top of them, before she scrambled into her own locker and closed hers.

Had they been spotted? She couldn't be sure.

All they could do now was wait and hope.

20

No Surrender

As Hanna struggled to make herself as comfortable as possible in the cramped, airless space, the dumb stupidity of what they'd just done struck home with the force of a sledgehammer. Now that power was restored, the security cameras would be working again, and they'd be spotted the moment they tried to get out of the boats. There was literally no way out. They might as well stand up, put their arms in the air and surrender.

Except, surrender was unthinkable! The Sea Wolf hadn't been joking when he'd described the death he'd got lined up for them. *A thousand cuts*! Just the thought of one cut, one slice carved from her body like a Sunday roast, was enough to make her blood run cold with terror.

As for a thousand of them . . .

She tried not to think about it; but it was impossible. Eventually they'd get caught. It was inevitable. One or other of them would give the game away—when cramp set in, or when hunger or thirst became unbearable. The Sea Wolf would get somebody else to do the actual cutting, she supposed. He'd just watch and laugh while it happened. She envied the boys squashed into their locker together. They might be uncomfortable, but at least they weren't left alone with their thoughts.

There were more voices now, people emerging from the main entrance tunnel, talking urgently to each other. Surely they weren't all needed to fix the generator? Hanna tried to make out what they were saying, but failed. If only she could understand Malay!

Despite the danger, she decided to risk a look. It was vital to find out what was happening. She took a deep breath, and praying that nobody would notice, slowly eased up the lid of her locker.

She had a surprisingly good view of the beach. A dozen or so men were gathered near the water's edge. More were joining them as she watched. She recognized them as the tough-looking, brown-skinned men she and the boys had passed on their way to the Sea Wolf's office earlier. They were dressed entirely in black and were heavily armed— most with automatic rifles, but several with hand-held rocket launchers. Grenades were hung from straps across their chests. Two of them were carrying tall bamboo ladders, and one had a large coil of rope slung from his shoulders. Hanna remembered the sign on the Sea Wolf's door: *Sea Wolf Shipping Protection Agency.* Presumably these men were the protectors.

But what ships were they protecting?

And from whom?

Soon afterwards, the Sea Wolf himself emerged onto the beach. He was limping badly and had a bandage round his head. He'd obviously come off worst in his tangle with the wild pigs. Hanna allowed herself a small smile of satisfaction.

He approached the men, and spoke to them curtly. Their leader, a tall man with a prominent hooked nose that made him look like an angry hawk, asked several questions, then unrolled a chart. The others clustered round to examine it closely. Judging by the way they were tracing across it with their fingers, it was showing some kind of route. The words *Ocean Spur* were repeated over and over again.

As quickly as it had begun, the briefing was concluded. The chart was rolled up and put away. The Sea Wolf disappeared back into the tunnel. The men checked their watches.

Then they turned and stared straight at Hanna.

Terrified, she jerked the lid of her locker shut.

Had they seen her?

She waited for shouts, footsteps. None came.

The realization hit her: they hadn't been

staring at her at all, but at the boats. Were they about to be launched?

The sound of the tractor starting up confirmed her theory. There was a series of violent jolts as Hanna's boat was hitched to it and dragged down into the water. The tractor returned for the boys' boat.

The men swung themselves on board. Hanna crouched in the darkness, her heart pounding. The initial burst of elation she'd felt at the thought of getting away from Big Pig Island had been replaced by sickening dread. The men would need somewhere to store their weapons. Any moment now the lid of her hiding place would be jerked open.

She'd attack them when it happened, she decided—try to claw their eyes out. If she was violent enough they'd be forced to kill her on the spot. Anything to avoid being slowly sliced to death!

A minute passed. Two. The worst minutes of Hanna's whole life.

Incredibly, the lid stayed shut.

There was a thump as somebody sat down on top of it, a creak as he adjusted his bottom to get comfortable. He clearly wasn't expecting to stand up again in a hurry! Hanna prayed that the boys were being as lucky as she was.

The huge engines growled into life. The boats

nosed out from the shore. Where on earth were they going?

It didn't matter, Hanna decided—allowing herself to relax a little—just so long as it was as far away from this cursed island and the evil man who controlled it as possible. Every second that passed felt like a second closer to freedom!

The voyage was smooth at first, the boat weaving out towards the open sea. But then the engines opened up with an ear-splitting roar.

It was like being in a heavyweight boxing match. Trapped in the dark, slammed against the rigid keel of the boat as each wave hit, Hanna felt as if every bone in her body was being smashed to pieces. She had a desperate urge to vomit—but she had nothing inside her to throw up. It had been so long since her last meal that she'd almost forgotten what food was.

Their speed increased by the minute. It was as if the boat had grown wings and was flying from wave-top to wave-top. Maybe being sliced to death wasn't so bad after all, Hanna thought. Anything except this brutal battering . . .

A bright sliver of light penetrated the locker. It died away, then came again. For a moment she was puzzled. Then she realized it must be the lighthouse she'd spotted from Big Pig Island earlier, when Jik had been saying his 'prayers'. Judging by the intensity of the light, they were passing quite close to it. To take her mind off the pain she was suffering, she forced herself to visualize the big map of the Sulu Sea that Dad had bought her after last year's adventure, and which she'd pinned up on her bedroom wall at home. Surely it must be possible to work out exactly where they were? She thought about the supply ship. After it had failed to stop at Puerto Princesa, it had headed due west for a whole day before it reached Big Pig Island. That meant the island must be quite close to the Borneo mainland. There was a deep channel running next to the coast, she remembered. Big ships used it. What was it called? She racked her brains.

The Balabac Channel! The lighthouse must be guarding its entrance. It could mean only one thing—they were heading out into the vast, shark-infested waters of the South China Sea . . .

The journey seemed to go on for ever. As time passed, Hanna lapsed into a strange semi-conscious state, somewhere between sleeping and waking. Vivid pictures flashed through her brain: home; school; the goats that lived in the lower field next to the cottage; her own little bed with its snuggly blue duvet.

Would she ever see any of them again?

After what seemed an eternity, the engine was suddenly throttled back, and the boat came to a halt. Judging by the long, slow rhythm of the waves, they must be far out in the ocean. Grateful for the respite, Hanna adjusted her body, trying to ease her battered limbs.

She felt a bump. The second boat had drawn alongside. It was weird to think of Jik and Ned crouched in the darkness just centimetres away from where she was—but comforting to know they were there.

The men were clearly nervous, calling out to each other, laughing over-loudly. They were waiting for something—but what?

A sudden sharp command. Then silence.

For a moment the swish and swirl of the waves was the only sound to be heard. But then came a new noise—a deep, slow rumble, like distant thunder.

There was a flurry of activity. A radio crackled. Once more Hanna caught the words *Ocean Spur*.

The man who'd been sitting on her locker stood up. He was jerking at something, making the boat tip. Dare she risk a look, she wondered? Would anybody notice if she lifted the lid just a fraction?

Taking a deep breath, she pressed her hands against it, eased it gently upwards, peered through the narrow gap she'd created.

Something very strange was happening. The

long coil of rope she'd seen one of the men carrying earlier was being quickly unwound. One end of it was fastened securely to the bow of their own boat. The other end was passed across to the second boat, and attached to *its* bow. The rope was carefully checked to make sure it would run freely, and there were no knots or tangles in its length.

The rumbling noise was getting louder by the second. Peering out across the waves, Hanna saw what looked like a huge, brightly-lit office-block heading swiftly towards them.

It was a ship—a very big ship—its masthead lights gleaming. The two boats were directly in its path. If they stayed where they were they'd be smashed to pieces!

Their engines roared into life, but the boats made no attempt to escape. The men were staring intently at the approaching ship, as if hypnotized by it. Hanna could hardly believe her eyes. Was this some kind of weird suicide pact?

On and on came the massive ship, holding its course and speed, taking no avoiding action. Clearly nobody on board it knew they were there.

It was a hundred metres from them now.

Fifty.

Thirty . . .

In those last terrifying seconds Hanna caught a glimpse of its name: *Ocean Spur*. She was screaming, but nobody could hear her. She sucked in a huge breath, ready to swim for her life.

21

No Hiding Place

Hanna braced herself for the impact, but it never came. Instead, a sharp order rang out, and with their engines howling, the two boats peeled swiftly away from each other—one to the left, the other to the right. The rope joining them jerked tight, whipping clear of the water.

As it did so, the ship hit it, like a runner going through a finishing tape.

Tipping crazily, the boats were dragged violently in towards the ship's sides. For one desperate moment, Hanna thought they were going to overturn, but they levelled out, and instantly their engines were cut. The ship was now towing them at high speed through the waves, their connecting rope stretched round its bow.

The whole manoeuvre had taken seconds. The skill had been extraordinary.

But there was no pause for congratulations. The men were pulling on balaclavas, checking their weapons. A ladder was swung up; hooked onto the ship's rail. The men swarmed up it onto the deck. Seconds later they'd disappeared from view.

It was a pirate attack—it had to be!

Hanna lifted her lid a little further and peered round. The boat was empty. They'd left nobody on guard. There was a real chance to escape, she suddenly realized. All she had to do was untie the rope that was towing the boats through the water. They'd be left behind as the *Ocean Spur* thundered off into the night, taking the Sea Wolf's men with it. But she must act quickly. The men could be back at any minute.

Her bruised limbs protesting, she hauled herself out of the locker and scrambled into the bow. Her heart sank. The rope was made from toughened nylon, stretched super-tight along the tanker's side. There was no way she could untie it—or cut it, without an axe or a knife.

Jik had a knife! He'd found one in the repair shop on Big Pig Island, she remembered, and had put it in his belt. Somehow she must get to the boys and they could cut themselves free.

But their boat was on the opposite side of the ship. To reach it, she'd have to cross the deck!

Pausing only to swallow a mouthful of water from a bottle one of the men had left behind, she swung herself onto the bamboo ladder and climbed upwards.

She peered cautiously over the edge of the ship. Its deck was enormous, stretching away into the far distance; a mass of pipes and valves. It was an oil tanker, she guessed, and judging by the way it was floating so low in the water, it must be fully loaded.

She'd come up close to the main superstructure, where the cabins were. Its great white walls, perforated with rows of gleaming windows, and topped by the bridge, soared up into the night sky. The upper section was brightly lit; but its base, where it joined the main deck, was in deep shadow. If she could reach it unseen, it would give her enough cover to cross to the other side of the ship.

It was now or never! She took a deep breath, vaulted the rail, and sprinted for the patch of shadow, all the time expecting to hear a challenging shout.

None came.

It was spooky, Hanna thought, as she reached safety and paused to look around her: there were fifteen—maybe twenty—armed men on board the ship, but it was as if they'd vanished into thin air. They must be hiding out of sight, waiting for orders to move in. The *Ocean Spur*'s crew were presumably still sound asleep, unaware of what was happening.

She crept cautiously forwards. In the centre of the ship, her route was blocked by a cluster of thick metal pipes. Some of them felt uncomfortably hot. A metal walkway passed above them. She was tempted to take it, but it was brightly lit and she would be dangerously exposed against the white walls of the superstructure.

Instead, she decided to squeeze underneath the pipes. If she made herself extra flat, like Ned had taught her, there might just be enough space to wriggle through.

It was like being in a highly uncomfortable obstacle race. Several times she gasped as her back came into contact with the hot metal casings of the pipes. Eventually she reached the other side and scrambled back into the shadows.

She'd stopped for a moment, getting her breath back, trying to work out exactly where the boy's boat would be, when she heard the voice. It was so faint she thought she must have imagined it.

It came again. *'Hanna?'*

She turned, her heart pounding. Two small black shapes were just visible behind her. It was Jik and Ned!

Almost hysterical with relief, she hurried to join them. They could so easily have missed each other in the darkness!

'Are you OK?' she whispered.

'Goddam hurting all over,' Jik's low voice came back.

'Me too. We've got to get out of here. I've got a plan!'

It was a great plan, Ned told her, after she'd explained it, except for one little thing. *The men had once more taken the ignition keys*. He'd checked before he and Jik had left their boat. Sure, they could cut the boats free, but if they couldn't start the engines, they'd be left floating helplessly in the middle of the ocean until they starved to death or died of thirst.

'We can always row,' Hanna said, bitterly disappointed.

'Don't be stupid!'

'Then what?'

There was silence as the children racked their brains, trying to think of something—*anything*.

Eventually Jik said, 'Maybe we don't need to escape.'

'Of course we've got to escape!' Ned exclaimed, horrified.

'Why? Nobody know we are here, so nobody come to look for us. We hide up somewhere and wait. When the Sea Wolf men finish and go away in their boats, we go to find the captain of this dam ship and tell him who we are. Then we get rescued for sure. Maybe they send goddam heli-copter to pick us up!'

He was right, Hanna realized. Staying put was the safest plan of all. If only every decision was this simple! All they had to do was find a safe place to hide.

But where?

The deck stretched away into the distance, as wide as a motorway, and just as exposed. Anybody glancing down from the bridge, or from any of the dozens of windows in the superstructure would spot them immediately if they ventured out onto it.

Staying where they were was equally impos-sible. The shadows that were concealing them would disappear the moment the sun rose.

Somehow they had to get *inside* the ship. There must be loads of places to hide in there.

Except . . . somewhere in the darkness the Sea Wolf's men were waiting. One false move, and it would all be over.

The children were still trying to decide what to do when a series of loud shouts made them glance sharply upwards.

High above them was the wing bridge, a brightly-lit open walkway stretching from the main bridge out to the sides of the ship. On it a desperate fight was taking place. One of the Sea

Wolf's men was wrestling with a white-uniformed figure. There was a flash of steel, a scream of agony. To the children's horror, the uniformed man pitched backwards over the rail and crashed down heavily onto the deck in front of them.

He was dead, blood oozing from deep stab-wounds in his chest.

Suddenly the Sea Wolf's men seemed to be everywhere, swarming up the external stairways, their black uniforms stark against the pristine whiteness of the ship. Most of them were clutching guns; several had knives drawn.

There were shouts, more screams. Doors were wrenched open and they disappeared inside.

Hanna, Ned, and Jik could only imagine the terror as the *Ocean Spur*'s crew were hauled from their beds, dragged downstairs and thrust onto the poop deck at the back of the ship. The men were screaming, crying, begging for mercy. It was the most terrible sound the children had ever heard. Even though they clamped their hands against their ears they couldn't block it out.

Then the shooting began.

Single shots at first. Followed by a barrage of gunfire as the automatic rifles opened up.

It can have lasted only a minute at the most, but it seemed to go on for ever, swelling in intensity until Hanna felt her brain was going to burst.

Then, mercifully, there was silence. Just the low rumble of the engines as the big ship butted onwards through the waves. It was as if even the executioners were stunned by what they had done.

The pause was brief. There were shouts, splashes, as the bodies were thrown overboard. Then came the pounding of feet as the killers fanned out across the ship. The children looked at each other in terror. Any moment now they would be spotted.

'The pipes!' Hanna hissed. 'Get under the pipes!'

They squirmed desperately beneath them. The boys made it, but Hanna's legs were still clearly in view when the first of the Sea Wolf's men rounded the corner.

Luckily he wasn't looking in their direction. He was concentrating on a door in the side of the superstructure. He wrenched at the handle, but it stayed firmly shut.

He didn't hesitate. He raised his gun and fired a short burst at the lock. Bullets whined off the tough steel plating.

A second man joined him. He too fired.

The door swung slowly open. 'Come out!' one of the gunmen bellowed in heavily-accented English. 'We know you are in there!'

If the men had shot open the door to a tiger's

cage, the reaction couldn't have been more sudden or more violent. A huge, muscular man, wearing just a pair of shorts, his whole body covered with intricate tattoos, exploded through the doorway. He was holding a thick iron bar. His eyes were glittering with fury. He was obviously prepared to take on every single one of his attackers.

He didn't get the chance.

There was a short burst of gunfire and he dropped to the deck clutching his abdomen.

More men arrived and he was pitched over the side. Whether he was alive or dead, it was impossible to say. The uniformed man who'd been killed earlier was thrown overboard after him. The killers disappeared inside the ship and the door clanged shut behind them.

'I feel sick,' Ned whispered, his voice unsteady. 'I think I'm going to throw up.'

'Well don't,' Hanna told him curtly.

She felt sick, too, but she refused to admit it—even to herself. They must stay calm, stay in control. She was staring at the damaged door. With no lock it should be easy to open.

But dare they go through it?

22

In Hiding

It was the coming of dawn that finally decided the children: a streak of pink in the east, strengthening and brightening by the second. Soon they'd be clearly visible to anyone who came on deck.

It would be suicide to stay where they were.

For hours they'd lain, spread-eagled underneath the pipes, all the time expecting the Sea Wolf's men to finish ransacking the ship and leave. Surely the pirates would want to be as far away as possible when daylight came?

Apparently not.

Not only had they shown no signs of departing, the *Ocean Spur* had altered course and was now heading north-east—Jik could tell that by looking at the stars. Where could they be going?

Wherever it was, it didn't much matter. Nothing mattered except finding a safe place to hide, and that had to be somewhere deep inside the ship. It was time to be brave.

Hanna glanced at the boys, gave them what

she hoped was an encouraging smile. 'Ready?' she whispered.

They nodded, their faces tight with anticipation.

'OK, let's go!'

Instantly they were up and running, aiming for the broken door. There was no way of knowing what lay behind it. They needed luck—lots of it.

It was the bosun's cabin—it was written on the door—and to their intense relief it was deserted. It had been badly trashed. The mattress on the high-sided bunk had been slit, its stuffing hanging out; the drawers underneath up-ended. Clothes and toiletries littered the floor.

There was a second door, directly opposite the first. It led into the interior of the ship. Cautiously the children pushed it open. Beyond it was a narrow corridor with several other doors leading off it. It was deserted. Judging by the noise, the pirates were on the floor above. They crept silently out into it.

Most of the doors had names written on them. One was marked Crew's Mess. Another, Cargo Control. A third, simply, Toilets. They eased them open and peered through. None of the rooms was any use as a hiding place. Hanna began to panic. How much longer would their luck hold out?

They'd almost reached the end of the corridor when a burst of laughter came from the floor above, followed by the thump of feet on a staircase. Somebody was coming down!

Ned quickly shoved open the nearest door. The children dashed through it, pulling it shut behind them.

They held their breaths. Had they been seen or heard?

The man reached the corridor and began to stumble along it. He seemed unsure of the layout of the ship. He paused outside the children's door. Horrified, they watched the handle turn . . .

Then, unexpectedly, it was released and the man lurched off down the corridor. A short while later there was the sound of running water. He'd been looking for the toilets! Hanna heaved a sigh of relief.

There were bolts on the inside of their door. She quickly shot them into place. Now, if anybody tried to get in, they'd assume it was locked. Feeling safer, the children looked around.

They were in the ship's laundry. Washing machines and tumble dryers lined one wall. Opposite was a sink with a draining board, and an ironing table. Scattered across the floor were cotton sacks full of what looked like bed sheets.

It was the perfect place to hide. Judging by the mess on the floor, the Sea Wolf's men had already been inside and checked it out. Now there was no reason for them to come in again. If you'd just hijacked a ship, the last thing you'd be thinking about was doing your weekly wash!

Most important of all, there was a tap. Hanna hurried across to the sink, turned it. Water gushed out.

Was it drinkable?

She rinsed out a plastic cup that had been used for measuring washing powder and filled it. She took a sip. The water certainly tasted clean. She handed it to the boys.

Jik drank first. Then Ned. Finally it was her turn.

She was about to refill the cup when a hiss from Ned stopped her. The man had finished in the toilet and was walking back along the corridor. It was impossible to know whether the sound of their tap running could be heard from outside, but it was foolish to take chances. The man disappeared upstairs again.

There was a single window giving a good view of the main deck. When she'd drunk her fill, Hanna hung a bed sheet in front of it to stop anybody looking in from the outside. Now, at last, they could relax a little—or at least they could have done, if it hadn't been for Ned.

'I'm hungry,' he announced. *'Starving!'*

'Me too,' Jik chimed in.

'You'll just have to put up with it,' Hanna told

them crossly. 'There's nothing to eat in here, unless you fancy some soap powder.'

'But it's ages since we've eaten anything!' Ned protested. 'Days! I can smell food. It smells really nice!'

Hanna sniffed. He was right. They must be quite close to the kitchen—what was it called in a ship? *The galley.* Somebody was frying something—chicken, it smelt like. 'Maybe we can get some food later,' she said tentatively.

'You mean steal some?'

She nodded. 'Tonight. When everybody's asleep.'

'But that's ages away!'

'Ned, please!' For a moment he'd turned back into her demanding, unreasonable little brother.

He realized it too. 'I'm sorry,' he said quietly. 'It's just hard, that's all.'

It *was* hard. Very hard. Even if you were a grown-up—even if you were the toughest man in the world—it would still be hard. In the last few hours they'd seen things—heard things—that happened only in nightmares.

But they'd been for real.

When she closed her eyes, Hanna could still hear the screams of the dying men, the thud of their bodies as they hit the deck, the sinister splashes as they were thrown overboard. Would

191

those sounds, those sights, ever leave her? She prayed that they would—and that in time, the boys would be free of them too.

Apart from the hunger that gnawed at them, the rest of the day passed quite pleasantly. They arranged the sacks to form mattresses, and fell asleep instantly, their battered bodies finally getting the rest they so badly needed. From time to time the sound of voices and footsteps outside their door roused them. But nobody attempted to come in, and they soon fell asleep again.

It was late afternoon when they finally woke. Something was different, Hanna realized as she sat up. It took her a while to work out what it was.

The engines had stopped.

The powerful rumble that had been ever-present since they'd boarded the ship had gone.

She went to the window, eased back the sheet, and peered out. They were still far out at sea, with no land visible.

Something was happening midway along the ship. She rubbed at the steamed-up glass to get a better view.

The big black inflatable boats they'd arrived in were being winched up onto the *Ocean Spur*'s deck. Why were the pirates doing that, she wondered? Surely they'd need them to get back to Big Pig Island?

She called the boys over. They were as puzzled as she was.

Their hunger grew worse. Hanna began to feel light-headed and unsteady. She knew they must eat soon or they wouldn't have the strength to escape—even if they had the opportunity.

As night fell the cooking began again. They could clearly hear the scrape-scrape of a spatula on a wok as something was stir-fried. There was a delicious, garlicky smell that reminded Hanna and Ned of Mum's cooking at home. It was like the worst form of torture!

The corridor outside filled with men. They were laughing, joking, smoking strange-smelling cigarettes. They obviously felt no guilt at the massacre they'd just carried out. They were heading for the Crew's Mess, next door to the laundry, which served as a dining room. The children had peeped into it earlier. Thank goodness they hadn't decided to hide in there!

After they'd eaten, the men stayed in the mess smoking and talking. Judging by the slap of cards, and the clink of money, they were gambling. Indonesian pop songs played loudly.

The evening seemed to go on for ever. At one point there was a loud argument—somebody was being accused of cheating, Jik said. Eventually chairs scraped back and the men began to leave, staggering upstairs in twos and threes. Finally—blissfully—there was silence.

Now was their chance!

The children forced themselves to wait for a while, to be absolutely certain that everybody was asleep. Then they slid back the bolts and opened the door.

The corridor was empty. The garlicky smell was much stronger now—mixed with the clove-like scent of the men's cigarettes. Following their noses, they tiptoed out.

The galley was three doors along, and it was unlocked. They slipped quickly inside. It was quite a big room, with several cookers, and a large stainless steel preparation table. It was too dark to see where the food was—but it didn't matter. All they had to do was sniff.

A wok was sitting on one of the stoves. Jik lifted its lid.

It was half full of *nasi goreng*—Indonesian fried rice. He was about to stick a hand into it, grab a mouthful, when Hanna stopped him. There'd be plenty of time to eat back in the laundry.

She ladled the rice into a plastic bag she found hanging near the stove. The cook was bound to realize the food had gone when he came into the galley in the morning, but with any luck he'd assume one of the men had got hungry in the night and had popped down for a midnight snack. The children crept out into the corridor, closed the door and scurried silently back to their hiding place.

The rice was utterly delicious. Sitting comfortably on the floor, they scooped out handfuls from the bag and stuffed it into their mouths. They were surprised at how quickly they felt full. During the long hours since their last meal, their stomachs must have shrunk.

They were washing down the rice with cups of water when a bell began to shrill. The three children glanced at each other in panic.

Had somebody raised the alarm?

Was the meal they'd just finished going to be their last?

23

Strange Arrivals

There were shouts and curses from the floor above. Feet pounded on the stairs. Hanna stared numbly at the laundry door. Any moment now it would be smashed open and their desperate adventure would be over.

It stayed shut.

Instead, the men hurried past and out onto the main deck. The ship's exterior lights flicked on.

The children crowded to the window to see what was happening. Approaching the *Ocean Spur*, their masthead lights gleaming, were two ships. As they got closer Hanna could see that the names on their bows were written in Chinese. They were tankers—much smaller than the *Ocean Spur*, maybe a third her size—riding high in the water; obviously empty. What on earth were they doing here?

They were brought skilfully to a halt, one on each side of the *Ocean Spur*'s main deck. Mooring ropes were thrown and made fast. Gangplanks were lowered, and uniformed men—presumably the captains of the Chinese tankers—clambered across onto the *Ocean Spur*.

Hurrying to meet them was the tall hawk-nosed man the children had last seen on Big Pig Island. There were handshakes. A brief conversation. Then signals were given to the crews, and flexible hoses were uncoiled, connecting the *Ocean Spur* to the newly-arrived ships. After a short pause, a loud mechanical throbbing began. For a moment Hanna was puzzled—but then she realized: it was the sound of pumps.

The *Ocean Spur*'s cargo was being off-loaded into the Chinese tankers! Thousands of pounds' worth of oil—*millions* of pounds' worth probably— was being stolen before their very eyes. Here was proof—if proof was needed—that the Sea Wolf was the biggest and most dangerous pirate of them all!

They watched the activity on the deck for a while, then returned to their sacks on the floor and lay down. The *Ocean Spur* was a big ship. Unloading would take a long time. With so many people about, there was no way they could do anything or go anywhere until the whole process was over and the Chinese vessels had gone.

But then what?

The unanswered question nagged at Hanna. What would happen when the *Ocean Spur* was finally empty? It couldn't just be abandoned. It was worth far too much money.

She'd read about hijacked ships in the chapter on pirates in her Borneo book at home. Usually their names were changed, their funnels were painted a different colour, and they were given fake ships' papers before being sold off cheap to crooked ship-owners. That must be what they were intending to do with the *Ocean Spur,* she decided.

If so, one thing was still clear: their best and only hope of survival was to stay exactly where they were. Eventually the *Ocean Spur* would have to go into port, if only to re-fuel. That was when they could make their escape.

Dawn broke, and still the unloading went on. Little by little the *Ocean Spur* rose in the water as her tanks were emptied. Soon only the superstructures of the Chinese ships were visible. Eventually even those sank downwards out of sight.

To pass the time, the children slept, or chatted in whispers. Hanna and Jik told Ned all about *The Dreamboat* and their adventures on board it. 'And all the time that was happening I was locked up in the dark!' Ned said ruefully, sounding quite envious. Jik found a pencil and paper on top of one of the washing machines and he and Ned played endless games of noughts and crosses. Jik usually won.

Towards evening the delicious aroma of cooking

returned. This time it smelt like fish and chips! Once again the Crew's Mess filled with men as they came in to eat.

The children's hunger flooded back—even worse than the night before. They'd been so stupid just taking the rice and not stopping for anything else, Hanna realized. There must be loads of other food stored away in the galley in cupboards and fridges. They could have brought back enough to keep them going for days. Now they'd have to make another raid—risk being captured all over again. And with all the activity happening on deck, tonight would be nowhere near as safe.

Once again, the evening seemed endless. But eventually the ship lapsed into a sort of silence, broken only by the throbbing of the pumps. People must still be awake supervising the unloading, the children supposed, but they'd be concentrating on what was happening on deck and not paying any attention to the galley. Now they knew exactly where to go, the three of them ought to be able to get there and back without being spotted.

All they needed was a little bit of luck.

They took a deep breath, eased open the door, and crept out into the corridor.

They'd almost reached the galley when they heard voices. The Crew's Mess wasn't deserted as they'd thought! At least two men were still inside it, talking in soft undertones. The children looked at each other in alarm. They should get back to the safety of the laundry immediately!

Yet they were so close to the food they desperately needed . . .

'Let's risk it,' Ned whispered.

Jik and Hanna nodded, scarcely daring to breathe.

They crept the last few metres to the galley and slipped inside, closing the door behind them as gently as they could. They stood in silence for a moment or two listening. There was no indication that they'd been seen or heard. Now all they had to do was locate the food!

With the deck lights shining in through the galley window, it was much easier to see than it had been the night before. There was a large fridge next to the preparation table. Ned opened it, but it was mostly full of milk and uncooked meat. There had to be other stuff somewhere else.

Jik found it. At the rear of the galley was a walk-in storeroom. It was full of boxes and cartons stacked on racks. The children read their labels with excitement. *Biscuits—Baked Beans—Breakfast Cereal—Tinned Ham—Spaghetti Hoops.* There was enough to feed an army. If they each took as much as they could carry, they wouldn't have to worry about food for days!

There were some empty cardboard boxes stacked in a corner. The children grabbed one each and quickly began to fill them. It was like being in a supermarket—except there was no checkout at the end. Ned found a carton of Jammie Dodgers, which were his favourite; and Jik actually discovered two boxes of Liquorice Allsorts! Soon their boxes were so full they could hardly carry them. Hanna went to a cutlery drawer and added a fork and spoon each—plus an all-important can-opener.

Clutching their loads tightly, terrified that they might trip and drop them, the children crept back to the galley door. They paused, listening intently for any suspicious noise from the corridor outside. There was none—even the conversation from the Crew's Mess seemed to have stopped. Whoever had been in there must have finally gone to bed.

Hanna lowered her box gently to the floor and reached for the door handle. She twisted it gently.

It wouldn't open.

Puzzled, she tried again, turning it more forcefully this time.

It still wouldn't budge.

'Let me do it!' Ned whispered exasperatedly, putting down his own box and pushing Hanna aside. 'It's dead easy! You just turn it to the left and . . . '

The door burst open.

Caught by surprise, the children were sent sprawling backwards across the galley. A blinding light flicked on. Three burly guards charged into the room, grabbing the children, jerking them to their feet. Hanna screamed in agony as her arms were wrenched up behind her back. She was propelled out through the door. Ned and Jik were dragged after her.

They were hauled up several flights of internal stairs, their heels banging painfully against the sharp metal steps. Eventually they reached the bridge, where they were thrown at the feet of Hawk-Nose.

He was supervising the last of the unloading, speaking urgently into an intercom. All around him dials and switches winked and glowed. The bridge looked more like a space station than something on a cargo ship.

He put down the intercom and glared at the children. 'Who are you? How did you get here?'

Hanna started to speak, but she was cut short by a guard. She recognized him as one of the men who'd been with them on their search for the Moon Pearl. His face still bore the cuts and bruises from his encounter with the wild pigs. He launched into a long tirade in Indonesian. Judging by the violence of his gestures, he was describing everything that had happened—including the roof-fall in the tunnel.

Hawk-Nose listened in silence, then he turned and keyed a number into a complicated-looking piece of electronic equipment. It was a satellite video-phone. After a short delay, a flickering image appeared on the screen.

It was the Sea Wolf! His snarls of rage echoed around the bridge as Hawk-Nose told him who they'd found. One at a time, the children were dragged in front of the camera. 'You will die!' the Sea Wolf screamed at them. 'You will die painfully! And you will die now!'

'We shoot them, boss?' Hawk-Nose asked uncertainly.

The Sea Wolf shook his head violently. 'Oh no! Where is the cook?'

A short, balding man stepped forward. He looked terrified. 'You know how to slice mutton?' the Sea Wolf demanded.

The cook nodded.

'Take these children to your kitchen and slice them in exactly the same way. Slice them slowly, until they are dead.'

The cook started to protest. 'I cannot . . . ' he began.

'Do it!' screamed the Sea Wolf. 'Do it, or you

will die the same death as these children! You have a video camera on this ship?'

'Yes.'

'Film it! I want to see everything! I want to hear their screams. I want to see the blood gush! I want to . . .'

There was a crackle, and the picture dissolved into a haze of static.

It didn't matter. The message was clear. 'You heard him!' Hawk-Nose snapped at the guards.

The children were dragged swiftly to the internal stairs. As she was hauled downwards, Hanna glanced out of the bridge window. The Chinese tankers had completed their loading and were moving slowly away from the *Ocean Spur*.

24

Blood!

Now Hanna knew what condemned men felt when they were being marched to the gallows. It wasn't fear, it was blind fury! As the three of them were half-carried, half-dragged from the bridge she screamed out in rage: kicking, biting; fighting the cruel arms that gripped her.

A fist crashed into the side of her head, making her ears sing, but still she struggled. She wouldn't die quietly! She utterly refused to give the Sea Wolf or anybody else the satisfaction of seeing her weep and beg for mercy.

The boys were fighting and yelling too. As they were dragged downwards, men gathered to watch on each landing, shouting out advice to the struggling guards as they passed, laughing loudly. It was like some kind of spectator sport.

The cook must have taken another route down from the bridge, because he was already in the galley when they arrived. He was setting up a small video camera on a tripod. It was pointed at the stainless steel preparation table. When he was satisfied that the focus was right, he opened a drawer, produced a vicious-looking Chinese cleaver and began to sharpen it. His hands were shaking, Hanna saw.

'Which one you want first?' Hanna's guard asked in broken English. There was a hint of excitement in his voice.

The cook, who Hanna guessed was a Filippino, ran his eyes over the children. He seemed to be trying to make up his mind. Then he said: 'All of them.'

The guard looked astonished. *'All of them?* At one time?'

He nodded. 'Leave them here. You go. I like to do this alone.'

'But if they escape?'

The cook felt the edge of his cleaver. It was now razor-sharp. 'They do not escape,' he said quietly. 'Now go. Close the door behind you. I call you when it is done.'

'We wait outside,' the guard said doubtfully.

'OK. You wait outside. Just go!'

Reluctantly, the guards did what they were told. There was disappointment on their faces. As the door clicked shut behind them, the cook locked it and turned swiftly to the children. 'My name is Pepe,' he said in an urgent whisper. 'I do not kill you. I cannot do this thing! I am a father. I have boy, girls, your age. But I must make like I kill you, do you understand?'

The children nodded numbly, not really understanding, but sensing that in some mysterious way, he was offering them a lifeline.

'You must scream,' Pepe said. 'You must scream loudly, as if I cut your bodies with my knife. You can do this thing?'

The children nodded again.

'OK. Do it!'

Hanna let out a long, warbling, high-pitched wail that made even her own blood run cold. Jik and Ned joined in. It was easy to make their screams sound genuine. All they had to do was glance at the cleaver glinting viciously in Pepe's hand and imagine it slicing into their flesh.

While they were screaming, Pepe took a large lump of raw meat out of the fridge, slapped it on a board and expertly cut it into numerous thin slices. 'Don't stop!' he whispered. 'Scream like you never scream before!'

The children obliged. They were suddenly—weirdly—beginning to enjoy themselves!

He turned to Ned. 'OK,' he ordered. 'You take off shirt. Get on table!'

Still screaming, Ned did what he was told.

Pepe swiftly arranged slices of meat across Ned's face and body. Then he dashed into the storeroom and emerged with a large plastic container.

It was tomato ketchup. Suddenly Hanna understood! She could have kissed the little bald-headed man.

Within seconds Ned looked as if he'd been the victim of a maniacal attack. Slices of what looked like his own living flesh were peeling away from his body, dropping from the table. More and more ketchup was slopped onto him. He appeared to be drowning in blood!

Hanna and Jik were ordered to lie down on the floor. Meat slices and ketchup were liberally splattered onto them too. It was like the aftermath of the worst massacre in the world. 'Now I film you,' the little man panted, half-covered in ketchup himself. 'Scream and scream, and then die. OK?'

'OK,' Hanna managed to gasp out.

The children performed brilliantly. As the camera whirred, Ned writhed on his table, coughing and choking, before slumping sideways, face down into a particularly large pool of ketchup. Hanna made as if she was trying to stand up, but then collapsed into a ketchuppy heap, her legs bent under her as if they'd been severed somewhere below her knees.

As for Jik, he continued to scream long after the others were 'dead', calling out for his mother in

Malay, dribbling ketchup from his mouth, before apparently passing out from loss of blood.

Pepe switched off the camera. 'Now you are dead, OK? You do not move, and you do not make noise. You do nothing until everybody is gone from this ship. Do you understand? I lock the door to keep you safe but there is another key in the store-room. May God be with you.'

He took the camera and opened the door. The guards were waiting outside. They peered in curiously, then recoiled. Even though they were brutal killers, what they saw obviously shocked them profoundly.

The door was swiftly closed again, Pepe's key twisting in the lock. Footsteps retreated in the direction of the bridge.

The children lay like corpses, hardly daring to breathe, listening to the pounding of their own hearts. Hanna had 'died' with her eyes open, and without turning her head she was able to see Jik who was sprawled next to her. He looked so wounded, so damaged, it seemed impossible that he was still alive. It was only when she tasted the 'blood' that was trickling down her face that she managed to convince herself that it really was just ketchup, and that all three of them were completely uninjured.

Her brain was racing. What had the cook

meant when he'd said they were not to move until everybody had gone from the ship? Surely if it was being hijacked, if it was being taken somewhere to be re-painted and disguised as a different ship, people would need to stay on board to steer it and operate its engines. Why would they all be leaving now?

There was a loud metallic hammering from somewhere, followed by the pounding of footsteps on the exterior stairways leading down to the main deck. Orders were shouted out. Something was happening outside—but what? Despite Pepe's warning, Hanna decided to take a look.

She was the closest of the three to the window that overlooked the deck. Memorizing her position in case she needed to return to it, she eased herself across and peered cautiously out.

The big, black inflatable boats were being lowered back into the sea. Hawk-Nose and the rest of the men were hurrying towards them. They were carrying something—it was difficult to see what. Hanna spotted Pepe amongst them. He was attracting curious glances. News of his 'massacre' must have spread rapidly round the ship.

It took a long time to launch the boats—they were heavy and awkward. Hawk-Nose seemed anxious, checking his watch constantly. When they were finally afloat, whatever it was the men were carrying was quickly loaded into them and the engines roared into life. The last of the pirates vaulted on board and the two laden boats curved swiftly away into the darkness.

The cook had been telling the truth, Hanna realized.

The *Ocean Spur* had been abandoned.

Now she and Jik and Ned were the only people left on board!

25
Alone

They found the key where Pepe had said it would be—hanging on a hook in the storeroom. Wiping off as much ketchup as they could, they unlocked the door and stepped out into the corridor. In the dull gleam from the bulkhead lights the children looked like three mangled corpses come back to life.

They stopped and listened. Apart from the slop-slop of the waves, and the creaking of the *Ocean Spur*'s hull, there was no sound.

They really *were* alone!

Ned turned uncertainly to the others. 'What do we do now?'

Jik was in no doubt. 'We go upstairs, call our mums and dads. No dam problem!'

Of course! The bridge! It was full of electronic stuff—full of ways of sending messages! Even if they couldn't get a phone to work, there was always the internet—or the radio. Hanna could imagine dialling up Mum's or Dad's number and getting straight through to their mobiles. How amazing it would be to hear their voices!

At last—at long last—they were going home! Soon this nightmare would be over, and they'd all be together again. 'What are you waiting for?' Ned yelled. 'I'll race you up top!'

It was a steep climb to the bridge, and the three of them were out of breath by the time they reached it. As they emerged into the large, brightly-lit wheelhouse, Hanna looked for the video-phone, through which the Sea Wolf had screamed his fury at them less than an hour earlier.

It was gone.

So were the computers, the radio telephone, and all the navigation equipment. Dangling wires showed where they'd been ripped from the control desk.

So *that* was what the men had been carrying when they'd gone back to the inflatable boats! No wonder the lockers had been left empty on the journey out—they were needed for the stolen goods.

Hanna stared at the devastation in despair. The *Ocean Spur* had been completely disabled. It was now just a floating hulk, drifting helplessly in the vastness of the South China Sea. There was no way of getting a message to the outside world.

The boys were as stunned as she was. Jik, she could see, was close to tears. She was trying to think of something—*anything*—that might get them out of this fix, when the lights suddenly went out.

Moments later the first explosion rocked the *Ocean Spur*.

At first she thought it was to do with the electricity—a generator blowing up or something. But then a second blast shook the ship. It was even stronger than the first.

'Look!' Jik was at the window, pointing down at the deck. Fires had broken out in two places near the bows, sending columns of smoke gushing up into the moonlit sky.

A third explosion followed. Then a fourth, directly beneath the superstructure. The children's ears sang as shock waves slammed into them.

Only then did they understand: the explosions were no accident. The Sea Wolf's men must have set the charges before they had left.

The Ocean Spur *was being deliberately sunk!*

There were two more explosions, the final one bigger than the rest, coming from the engine room at the rear.

The huge ship gave a sudden shudder, like a dog shaking itself, and tilted sideways. The children looked at each other, wild-eyed.

'We've got to get out of here!' Ned gasped.

'But how?' Hanna asked frantically.

'Use lifeboats!' Jik yelled.

There were two lifeboats—large orange-coloured craft slung from davits on either side of the ship. It ought to be possible to reach them if they were quick.

The ship gave another violent lurch and keeled over further, knocking Hanna off her feet, sending her slithering wildly across the floor. Jik and Ned clung desperately to the chart table to stop themselves joining her. The bridge was already beginning to hang dangerously out over the sea. They must get to the lifeboats before the whole ship turned over!

Hanna glanced at the internal stairs, the ones they'd just come up. They could go down those—but the thought of being trapped inside the ship if it suddenly sank was so dreadful she dismissed the idea. They must aim for the far door, the one that led out onto the wing bridge and the external stairways.

Normally they would have reached it in seconds—but not now. As the angle of the ship had steepened, the door had risen high above their heads. Grasping at anything they could find, using every drop of their strength, they hauled themselves up towards it. It was like climbing a slippery

215

mountain. *Please don't tip any more!* Hanna begged the doomed ship. *Please stay right where you are!*

Jik reached the door first and gripped its handle. But it opened outwards, and there was no way he could shift it. Could the three of them, heaving together, manage to do it?

They could—just! It swung back with a loud crash.

The children scrambled out into the open air.

It was then—and only then—that they realized just how terrifying their predicament was. The *Ocean Spur* was sinking fast, each lurch tipping it further and further over. In minutes it would be gone!

Coughing in the acrid smoke that was billowing from the shattered tanks, the children swung themselves onto the external stairs, and using the rails and posts as hand-holds, half-climbed and half-slid downwards. Below them, part of the main deck was already awash.

They reached one of the lifeboats, but it was far too heavy for them to handle, even if they'd known how to launch it. They were trapped!

Hanna's terrified eyes sought the boys'. If the ship sank they would be sucked down with it, however hard they tried to swim.

Ned glanced round wildly. 'There's something else,' he exclaimed. 'I don't know what it is, but I

216

think it might be for life-saving. Jik and I saw it when we first came on board. It's got *"Twelve Persons"* written on it.'

'Where is it?' Hanna demanded, her hopes suddenly soaring.

'Follow me!'

Following Ned was easier said than done. The *Ocean Spur* was now almost flat in the water, and the children found themselves scrambling across what had once been the sheer outer walls of the superstructure. 'There!' Ned yelled, pointing.

The 'thing' looked exactly like the gas tank in the garden at home, except it was made of plastic not metal. Quite how it could save anybody's life, Hanna couldn't work out. Maybe it was just meant to float and you held onto it—still, anything was better than nothing!

It was held in a sort of cradle by two straps. They were surprisingly easy to undo—just a quick flick released them. Now all they had to do was get it into the water.

For something so big, it was extremely light. Heaving together, the children managed to roll it out of its cradle and over the edge of the deck. It thumped down the ship's side, and into the sea.

It was attached to the cradle by a long rope. Ned jerked at it.

That was when the miracle happened.

There was a loud hiss and the cylinder split in half. Thrusting out of it, writhing like a sea-monster as it filled with air, was a large circular life-raft, black at the bottom, luminous orange on top. A conical roof rose up to cover it.

They were still staring at it in amazement when the *Ocean Spur* gave another massive lurch. It was about to turn completely over! Terrified they would be trapped underneath, the children swung themselves desperately over the rail and tumbled down into the water. 'Swim!' Ned shouted. 'Swim like anything!'

The raft had been caught by the wind and was being blown quickly away from the ship. Only its rope was holding it back. If it was going to save them, the children would have to reach it, get on board, and cut the rope. If not, it would be dragged down by the ship when it sank.

Swimming like she'd never swum before, Hanna powered towards it. Ned followed close behind. Jik had landed in the water much further away. He too was swimming towards the raft at top speed—but would he reach it in time? The *Ocean Spur* was groaning and hissing like a huge, dying animal. It had only seconds to live.

Jik was tiring now, his arms flailing. 'Don't stop!' Hanna screamed at him as she and Ned reached the raft.

She stretched herself out to Jik, urging him onwards.

Her hands found his, and she pulled him towards her, almost hysterical with relief. There was an opening into the raft with a sort of step underneath. Using it, Ned flung himself on board. Jik tried to join him but the raft tipped violently. It looked as though it might flip over completely.

'Go to the other side!' Hanna screamed at her brother. 'You've got to balance us!'

Ned threw himself across the raft, leaning his weight out as far as he could. It worked! Jik hauled himself up and scrambled in.

Hanna was still in the water when the *Ocean Spur* began to sink. It happened so fast she scarcely had time to cling on to a handhold before the raft began to be pulled violently through the waves towards it. 'Cut the rope!' she screamed at Jik. 'Cut it now!'

But he had no knife. The pirates had taken it when they'd been captured. He tried to bite through the tough nylon line, but it was impossible.

Then, just when it looked as if they were going to be dragged down to their deaths, Ned spotted a knife. It was in a reinforced pocket next to the raft door. He slid it out and hacked frantically at the line.

219

One strand parted.

And a second.

Finally the last strand gave way with a loud twang.

The children watched in horror as the bows of the *Ocean Spur* rose up high above them. Slowly at first, then with increasing speed, spewing smoke and water from its crippled hull, the huge ship slid stern-first beneath the waves and was gone.

26

Adrift

For a few terrifying moments it looked as if the raft would be sucked into the swirl of burning oil and floating debris that marked the place where the *Ocean Spur* had sunk. But then Ned discovered the paddles.

There were two of them, attached to the side of the raft. He swiftly unhooked them, threw one to Jik. The boys thrust them into the water. Slowly they drew clear. Hanna heaved a sigh of relief. If they'd hit the burning oil, the raft would have gone up in flames.

After a while the boys stopped paddling. A breeze had picked up and was now blowing them further and further away from the site of the shipwreck. Hanna scanned the horizon. It was empty. There was no sign of land—or of any ships.

But for now, that didn't matter. They'd survived!

There was a large blue bag in the raft, a bit like a sports bag. Ned unzipped it. It was full of stuff, including plastic bags of water, and something called *Seven Oceans Standard Emergency Rations For Lifeboats,* which presumably was food. There were also some flares, a torch, and a small hand-held radio transmitter. Ned ripped the radio out of its case, pressed a switch and put it to his mouth. 'Mayday!' he bellowed into it. 'Mayday! Mayday! SOS!'

There was no response. Looking at it, it seemed obvious why: the batteries powering it were badly corroded. Bitterly disappointed, he flung it overboard. 'It was our only chance!' he yelled at Hanna, as if she was personally to blame for it not working.

'Of course it wasn't our only chance!' she retorted. 'This raft is for twelve people—twelve *grown-ups*. There's only three of us in it and we're children. That means we've got enough food and water to last us for days—weeks if we're careful. There's even a fishing line so we can catch fish. The South China Sea is one of the busiest shipping areas in the world. I know that because Dad told me so! We'll get picked up soon.'

Ned peered at the empty horizon. 'By whom?'

Hanna felt like hitting him, he was being so infuriating. 'By a ship! There's probably hundreds of them heading towards us right now. When we see one, all we have to do is fire one of these rocket things and it'll stop!'

'Oh yeah?'

'*Yes!*'

'Holy Moses, please stop making goddam argument!' Jik pleaded. 'We are dam lucky to be alive! We should be thanking our stars.'

'Lucky stars,' Ned corrected.

'I don't care what sort of dam stars! You are being like babies!'

Hanna and Ned calmed down. Jik was right. They *were* lucky to be alive. Very lucky. Arguing would get them nowhere.

It was hunger, Hanna guessed. And fatigue. 'We could try some of these emergency rations,' she suggested.

'They look gross,' Ned said. 'They've probably been in that bag for years.'

They may have looked gross, but they were surprisingly tasty—and quite fresh inside their foil wrappings. They were like big soft biscuits. They ate one each and washed them down with some of the water. They felt better almost immediately—and a lot less irritable with each other.

Still no ships.

The South China Sea was big, Hanna knew, but surely there ought to be at least *one* ship in sight somewhere on the horizon?

Then she remembered: after it had been hijacked by the Sea Wolf's men, the *Ocean Spur* had changed course and headed north-east. That must have been to take it away from the busy shipping lanes. The pirates had wanted no witnesses when its cargo was stolen and it was blown up and sunk.

No wonder there were no ships around!

Jik didn't seem worried. He wetted his finger and held it up above his head. 'No dam problem!' he announced. 'We got good *habagat*—good wind. It blow us back to the south, where the ships are. Now we relax, put goddam feet up!'

Which is precisely what he proceeded to do.

Ned joined him, sprawled comfortably in the bottom of the raft. Moments later, the two of them were fast asleep.

Hanna didn't join them. One of them should be awake at all times, she knew. A ship could easily pass close by without them seeing it—or it seeing them.

They must divide the day into watches, she decided. She'd do the first, then she'd wake up one of the boys to take over from her. If only they had a clock! Without one it was so difficult to know how much time had passed.

She tried to keep awake—she really tried. But gradually exhaustion, and the gentle rocking of the raft, lulled her, and her eyelids began to droop. A good snooze was just what the doctor ordered, she found herself thinking—and anyway, there were no ships for miles around . . .

She was so wrong!

What seemed like just minutes later she woke to the loud rumble of engines. A huge ship, its decks piled high with containers, was cruising past them at high speed. It was very close—no more than a couple of hundred metres away. 'Stop!' Hanna yelled, standing up and waving her hands frantically above her head.

The boys woke up and were on their feet in an instant, joining in. The ship *must* slow down!

It didn't.

They could see the people on its bridge. They were talking to each other, staring straight ahead. *'Look at us!'* Hanna bellowed at them, stupidly, uselessly. *'Just look at us!'*

'Get a flare!' Ned yelled. 'We must let off a flare!'

Hanna scrambled for the bag, emptied it out. There were three flares. They were all different, and had instructions written on them.

But there was no time to find out how they worked. The ship was already past, and receding quickly into the distance. Even if they managed to fire one, nobody on board was likely to see it.

The children sank down, bitterly disappointed. But at least it was a ship. Where there was one ship, there'd be others. Next time they must be ready.

Ned laid out the flares in a row and read out what was written on them. One was hand-held, and worked like a posh firework. The second was a smoke flare which produced orange smoke when it hit the sea. The third was a parachute flare. It consisted of a rocket with a little parachute inside it, which kept a bright light floating in the sky for up to thirty seconds after it was fired. Operating them looked easy. All you had to do was unscrew a plastic cap, aim them downwind away from the raft, and pull a firing loop.

The big container vessel must have been way off course, because for the rest of the morning, and throughout the long afternoon that followed, the children saw only one more ship—and that was so far away on the horizon there was no point in trying to signal to it. Where on earth were all the others?

As the day wore on, it got hotter and hotter. The store of drinking water looked so tempting—but there were no arguments when Hanna insisted on rationing it. They'd need at least a litre a day in this kind of heat, she knew; but they'd have to make do with less. She worked out that they had about ten days' supply. They shared a biscuit for lunch, and put aside another one for later. Jik unwrapped the fishing line—it had a silver spinner on one end—and he and Ned spent a long time trying to catch supper, but without success. They must watch out for flocks of seabirds, Jik said. That was where the fish were.

Towards evening they spotted some islands in the distance—anonymous humps, crowned with straggly palm trees. There was no way of reaching them, even though the boys got out the paddles and tried. They soon faded from view. It was probably better being out at sea, Hanna decided, rather than being stranded on some distant reef.

Then they saw the Russian ship.

They were dividing up their evening biscuit when Ned spotted it. It was heading straight towards them. They didn't know it was Russian until it had passed them and they could read the name on its stern, which said it was from St Petersburg. It had a lot of cranes on its deck and no flags flying.

They decided to use the hand flare. There was a brief argument between Jik and Ned over who should fire it, which Jik won. The children waited excitedly for the ship to get close enough. They must make no mistake this time!

'I fire now?' Jik asked, squirming with impatience.

'No, wait!' Hanna exclaimed. There was nobody in the wheelhouse—or at least, nobody she could see. It must be on auto-pilot.

Then she spotted a man. He was out on the wing bridge, smoking a cigarette. 'OK, fire!' she yelled.

Jik unscrewed the cap, aimed the flare away from the raft, and pulled the trigger loop. There was a loud hiss. Red flame and smoke shot into the air. It only lasted a few seconds, but it was dazzlingly bright.

The ship didn't stop.

The man had seen them, Hanna was certain of that, because he threw away his cigarette and went quickly into the wheelhouse. Seconds later there was a deafening hoot from the ship's siren. The children watched open-mouthed in disbelief as it sped past them without changing course, and disappeared into the evening haze.

Ned was in tears. 'He saw us! I know that man saw us!'

'That's why he make that dam hooting noise,' Jik said, equally devastated. 'Holy Moses, he laugh at us! He think it is funny!'

'Maybe it was a spy ship,' Hanna suggested. 'A lot of Russian ships are. That man would probably have been shot if he'd stopped to help us.'

'You've been watching too many films,' Ned told her bitterly.

They saw several more ships before night fell. None of them stopped. The first of them, a small Vietnamese freighter loaded with planks of wood, almost collided with them as it rumbled past. They fired the orange smoke flare, and Ned was about to fire the parachute flare when he stopped himself. 'We should save this one for later,' he said. 'We might need it really badly.'

There was little doubt now: they were being deliberately ignored. Were they just going to be left to drift until they ran out of water and died? Surely there was a law about stopping to pick up survivors at sea?

It was only after yet another large container ship had disappeared over the horizon that the truth finally occurred to Hanna: these were pirate-infested waters. Ships' captains must be under orders not to stop for anybody or anything.

'Maybe we'll see some fishing boats,' Ned ventured. 'They'll stop for us, I bet.'

'Not many fishing boat come here,' Jik said glumly. 'Is too much danger. Holy Moses, if only this goddam raft have sail, then we can get somewhere!'

'We can paddle,' Hanna suggested.

'No dam good! We just go backwards every

time the wind blow, every time a wave come. This thing is not like boat. It is like . . . '

'A bouncy castle?' Ned suggested.

'Goddam castles don't bounce!' Jik protested.

Hanna and Ned spent some time trying to explain to Jik exactly what a bouncy castle was, and what it was used for; but he still didn't seem any the wiser.

Eventually they gave up. It was too painful to talk about things from home—things they might never see again. After that, they lapsed into silence, each of them lost in their own thoughts.

Hanna had just decided that they must reduce the amount of water they drank each day, try to make it last longer, when she felt a bump. It was quite a big bump, jolting the whole raft, throwing her off balance. 'Cut it out, you two!' she snapped at the boys, assuming they were fooling about.

'It wasn't us!' they protested loudly.

There was a second bump, this time from a different direction. It was coming from *outside*, she realized.

'What is it?' Ned asked in a scared voice.

Hanna groped in the bag for the torch, switched it on. Thank goodness *it* worked! Could it be dolphins, she wondered? They were always very playful. Maybe they thought the raft was some kind of outsized beach ball. She crawled to the doorway, and shone the torch down into the water, expecting to see their smiling, friendly faces.

There were no dolphins.

Instead, circling the raft, occasionally butting at it with its nose, was the biggest shark she'd ever seen.

27

Terror in the Night

It was a tiger shark—the stripes on its massive body were clearly visible. Hanna recognized it at once from the chart Ned had on his bedroom wall at home. It was one of the most aggressive and dangerous sharks of all, attacking and eating anything and everything that came its way—dolphins, turtles, seals—even things like motor tyres and petrol cans! And of course people. Lots of them. Only the great white shark was a bigger killer.

Nothing the Sea Wolf had threatened them with could compare to the desperate terror she felt at that moment. She threw herself back inside the raft, drawing her knees tightly up to her body.

'What did you see?' Ned asked in a quavering voice.

Hanna tried to reply, but she could hardly speak. It was as if somebody was gripping her throat, strangling her. 'Shark!' she just managed to gasp. 'Tiger shark!'

'Holy Moses!' Jik exclaimed. 'Now we are in *big* dam trouble!'

There was another bump. This time harder, more aggressive. It was sizing them up, Hanna guessed, deciding whether to attack. From underneath, the raft must look like a turtle—a giant black turtle. Big marine turtles were the tiger shark's favourite food, she remembered Ned telling her. They had teeth specially designed to cut through the toughest shells. Well this particular turtle didn't have a shell—just a thin rubber skin filled with air. One bite—one single bite—was all that was needed!

The children clung together in the centre of the raft, waiting, praying. Was it a good sign that it hadn't attacked yet? Perhaps it had already eaten. Perhaps it was just being nosy, filling in a few spare minutes between meals. Perhaps it would just go away . . .

It didn't.

The shark attacked with a suddenness and swiftness that took them all by surprise. It came in at an angle, twisting as it approached. It was like being hit by a train.

Its jaws clamped down on the side of the raft. There was a loud hiss as its teeth punctured the casing, and the compressed air inside began to escape.

Alarmed, the shark backed off.

But not for long.

It came in again, even more aggressively, gripping the crippled raft, shaking it like a dog shakes a slipper. Only the roof was still inflated, and two or three panels at the back.

The children clung desperately to anything they could find, knowing instinctively that staying with the raft was their only hope. Even a shark this big couldn't swallow the whole thing in one gulp.

It was getting angry now, wrestling with the slippery, flapping rubber, ripping great gashes in it. It tried to dive, but the raft wrapped itself round its head, forcing it back to the surface again.

Once more it backed off. For the first time since the attack had begun, Hanna could see it clearly. It was looking at her, she realized—looking straight at her! It was like peering into the eyes of the devil himself.

It came in yet again. This time it had learnt its lesson. It ignored the raft and went straight for the children, hurling itself at them, its jaws locked open, its rows of razor-sharp teeth gleaming in the moonlight. Hanna twisted back, desperately trying to get away from it.

As she did so, there was a flash, and something shot past her ear. For an instant it seemed as if the whole of the shark's interior was on fire, burning with an intense red light.

Then its huge jaws snapped shut, and with an immense splash, it disappeared.

She turned to her brother. Ned was clinging to the remains of the raft with one hand. With his other he was gripping the parachute flare launcher.

The flare was gone.

'Oh my God!' Hanna heard herself saying, as the shock hit her. 'Did you fire that thing at it?'

Ned nodded. He was sobbing uncontrollably. 'It went right inside . . . '

'Raft is broken!' came Jik's anguished cry. 'Goddam shark bite through every dam bit!' The Sea Gypsy boy was braced against the last of the inflated panels, his hand pressed to a jagged rip in its cover.

It was hopeless. The air was hissing out violently between his fingers. In a matter of seconds it would be gone. They had no lifejackets, and no other means of support. Soon they'd be swimming for their lives, trying to stay afloat, knowing that where there was one shark, there would be others, attracted by the sounds and smells of the struggle that had just taken place.

'Stay together!' Hanna yelled, as the crippled raft finally sank beneath them.

She reached out, found Ned's hand. Jik gripped her other one. They formed a circle, their feet pressed together in the centre. The next time a shark attacked, there wouldn't be any warning, she knew. Every breath they took—every beat of their hearts—could be their last . . .

They didn't hear the engine, or see the lights. They were too busy trying to stay afloat, trying to keep their mouths and noses clear of the wave crests that were breaking all around them.

There were splashes. One. Two. Three.

Brown bodies speeding towards them.

An arm looped round Hanna's waist, supporting her, lifting her head clear of the waves. For a brief moment she struggled, not wanting to let go of the boys, but she was prised away from them.

Was what was happening real, or just a vicious trick being played on her by her exhausted brain? It was impossible to tell.

She turned her head.

Next to her was a familiar face with its weird empty eye-socket.

It was the Maestro!

Behind him, its engine throbbing softly, was *The Dreamboat*, its rail lined with excited small boys.

'We must be quick!' the Maestro said to her urgently in his deep, strange voice. 'There are many shark here! You can swim?'

Hanna nodded. Her anxious eyes sought Ned and Jik, but she needn't have worried. Crew members had reached them too, and they were being escorted swiftly towards the ancient ship.

'Shark! Shark!'

They'd just reached *The Dreamboat* when a frantic shout rose up from the dive boys on the deck. They were pointing at the water.

Hanna glanced behind her. An enormous dorsal fin had broken the surface and was heading swiftly towards her. With the last of her strength, she grabbed a knotted rope hanging down the ship's side and hauled herself upwards. Willing hands stretched out for her, and she was dragged over the rail, onto the familiar, slippery, fish-stained deck.

28

Decisions

'I do not believe it!'

Nina was waddling towards them as fast as her stumpy legs could carry her, arms outstretched. 'I do not believe it is you! I think you are a vision sent by the blessed Santo Nino!'

'We're real!' Hanna just managed to say before she was squashed into the fat woman's enormous bosom.

It was extraordinary, unbelievable, wonderful! When Hanna finally managed to surface for air, she saw that the dive boys had formed a circle round them, dancing and clapping.

'Here's Jik!' Nina exclaimed, wrapping him in her arms in turn. 'And who is this?'

'This is Ned—my brother. He was lost in the storm, remember? We found him.'

Ned backed away nervously, but there was no escape. He too was crushed in a massive hug.

'I bring food!' Nina said, releasing him, wiping tears from her eyes. She went swiftly to the kitchen and emerged with a large bowl of rice and fish, and a plastic jug of water. 'Come, eat!' she said, gesturing for them to sit.

The children slumped down onto the deck. They were thirsty, rather than hungry—they'd swallowed a lot of seawater when the raft had sunk—and they drank deeply from the jug, not caring about the stale metallic taste of the water inside it. They followed it up with a mouthful or two of rice, just to please Nina. The crew and the dive boys crowded around them, not wanting to miss a thing.

They were joined by the Maestro. He seemed to have completely recovered from the jellyfish attack—though his bare chest was still criss-crossed with livid scars.

'This place is called Tiger Shoal,' he said. 'There are many shark here. It is very good fortune we hear your signal and come to search for you. If not you are dead.'

'What signal?' Hanna asked.

'We hear SOS signal on radio. "*Mayday Mayday SOS!*" It give your position also.'

So the radio transmitter Ned had thrown overboard had been working after all! Hanna glanced at her brother. He looked suitably ashamed of himself.

She turned back to the Maestro. 'You saved our lives,' she said gratefully.

His single eye shone. 'Now we are even, huh? Now we are for ever friends!'

Hanna nodded. 'For ever!' And to think she'd once hated this strange, ugly man! But she was puzzled. 'What are you doing here? This is the South China Sea.'

'We come to catch fish,' Nina told her. 'There are big reefs close to this place. We catch many, but then Chinese gunboat come. They say it is their reefs, their fish. They point big gun at us, so we must go away. I spit on them! But you must tell us why *you* are here. We think you are safe home with your mother and father!'

'It's a long story,' Ned said.

It *was* a long story. Hanna began to tell it, with Jik and Ned joining in from time to time. Nina translated for the benefit of the crew and the dive boys. The Maestro reacted with fury when he heard how the children had been sold to the Sea Wolf. 'I hear about this Sea Wolf,' he said. 'He is very powerful man. He have many important friends. Everybody is afraid of him. Only the Datuk is more powerful.'

'He *is* the goddam Datuk!' Jik exclaimed.

There was a stunned silence. 'You tell the truth?'

'He told us himself,' Ned put in. 'He was going to kill us, so he had no reason to lie.'

'But this Sea Wolf is white man. Datuk is Malaysia man.'

Hanna explained about the plastic surgery; the skin lightening.

It was as if a trigger had been pulled. Without warning, the Maestro's face changed. It became distorted with rage, foam oozing from the corners of his mouth. 'I kill him!' he shouted. *'I kill him!'*

Nina got to her feet, rushed to his cabin. She returned with a cup of brown liquid. 'Drink this!' she ordered.

For a terrifying moment it looked as if he would refuse, but then he gulped it down.

The effect was immediate. He shook his head as if to clear it; glanced at the children. 'I have big sickness in my brain,' he said hesitantly. 'Sometimes . . . '

'We know,' Hanna replied softly. 'We do not judge you.'

'You do not judge me?' The shine had returned to the Maestro's eye. 'You are good children. You are best children in the world! You will help me to find this Datuk Sea Wolf? I have been hunting him for so many months!'

Now it was Nina's turn to react with anger. 'You cannot ask these children to do this! It is big danger! They must return to their mothers and fathers immediately. You must radio to coastguards. Tell them we rescue them from the sea. They must go home right now!'

The Maestro hesitated. Hanna could almost *see* the struggle that was taking place in his injured brain. Eventually he seemed to reach a decision. 'OK. They go home! I do not need them! I know where is this Big Pig Island. Somehow I find this Sea Wolf. Somehow I kill him. No problem!'

He got to his feet, heading for the wheelhouse. He was lurching badly. The medicine was clearly affecting him.

'He's crazy!' Ned exclaimed. 'If he goes anywhere near Big Pig Island without knowing what he's doing, he'll be killed—and so will anybody who goes with him! The Sea Wolf's men have got guns, grenades—even rocket launchers. He won't stand a chance! We've *got* to help him!'

'But what about Mum and Dad?' Hanna asked, anguished. 'They've been waiting for us for so long!'

'They can wait a little bit longer!'

'Ned say the truth!' Jik put in. 'If we let the Sea Wolf win this time, many more dam ships get attacked. Many more people die!'

The boys were right—Hanna knew it in her heart of hearts. If they went back now, she knew exactly what Dad would do. He'd insist on contacting the Philippine authorities, insist that action was taken. The moment he did that, somebody would warn the Sea Wolf and he would escape once again. 'OK, we'll stay,' she said finally. 'We'll help the Maestro. But we must *capture* the Sea Wolf—not kill him. We mustn't kill anybody, however wicked they are!'

'And how exactly *do* we capture him?' Ned demanded.

'I don't know. We'll think of something. But we'll have to be very clever. Cleverer than we've ever been before!'

There were noises from the wheelhouse. A loud crash. Jik scrambled to his feet. 'We must stop Maestro or he radio to coastguards!'

He raced up to the bridge, only to emerge moments later with a grin on his face. 'He is asleep on floor!' he announced. 'No dam problem!'

The children slept soundly that night—Hanna in her familiar fish-net hammock, the boys on mats on the kitchen floor. It was as if they'd come home. They woke next morning to the sounds of the Maestro singing cheerfully as he sluiced himself down with seawater from a bucket. Someone must have told him about their decision to stay, Hanna supposed. She hoped—desperately—that it was the right one.

It was a glorious day. The sun shone down from a cloudless sky. The sea was a deep transparent blue, sparkling in the intense light. Glancing over the side as she ate her breakfast rice, Hanna saw a dorsal fin break the water—and another. This time it really *was* dolphins! There was a whole pod of them, leaping and diving all around *The Dreamboat*'s bows. It seemed unbelievable that this same calm sea had threatened them with such violent deaths only hours earlier.

Mid-morning they anchored off a small island and everybody went ashore in the dive boats. It was a holiday, the Maestro said, to celebrate the children's safe return. The dive boys shinned up the palm trees that hung over the beach and cut down enough green coconuts for everybody. Their milk was delicious—as was the tender white flesh they scraped from their insides.

It was wonderful being at peace—if only for a day. Hanna, Jik, and Ned joined in with the dive boys as they played hide and seek in the dense scrub that covered the island. For the first time, Hanna got to know all their names—Pen, Jun, Tibo, Kokoy, Kalbo . . . There were so many of them!

The Maestro brought lines and he and the crewmen caught large numbers of reef fish which they split open and roasted on a driftwood fire for lunch. They were delicious! Nina found a comfortable seat in the shade of a large fig tree and kept a watchful eye on proceedings.

The boys had brought their catapults, and after they had eaten they spent a long time on target practice, trying to hit a floating coconut way out in the lagoon. They were amazingly accurate, with hardly any misses.

The Maestro and his men went to sit with Nina in the shade. They called Hanna, Ned, and Jik across to join them. Their discussion lasted throughout the heat of the afternoon, and into the early evening. By the time they'd finished, the shadows had grown long, and their plans had been made.

29

The Battle of Big Pig Island

They were further north than Hanna had realized, and it took a full day's cruising before *The Dreamboat* finally reached the Balabac Channel. As the sun began to set, the flashes from the lighthouse became clearly visible. Just beyond it lay their destination—Big Pig Island.

The children joined the Maestro and one of his crewmen—a cheerful little man called Ernesto—in the wheelhouse. While Ernesto steered, the Maestro scanned the horizon with a pair of battered binoculars.

He was looking for a ship. Any ship.

'Always there are ships here!' he grumbled. 'Always! Why not today when we are needing one most?'

He was thriving on the tension, Hanna saw. He looked more alive than she'd ever seen him before.

It was almost dark before they sighted a ship. It was an ancient, rusting freighter that looked nearly as old as *The Dreamboat*. Chained to its deck was a cargo of second-hand tractors.

They were in luck. It was heading for the deep-water channel that ran past Big Pig Island, and it was travelling slowly. Any faster, and *The Dreamboat*'s clapped-out engines might not have been able to keep up with it.

It was Ned's idea to find a passing ship and shadow it closely as they approached the island. That way there'd be less chance of their being spotted from the shore. If the ship was big enough, *The Dreamboat* could stay hidden behind it almost the whole way in. Even more importantly, there'd be just a single blip on any radar screen, instead of two.

With enormous skill Ernesto brought *The Dreamboat* alongside the freighter, leaving just two or three metres between them. For several minutes there was no response from the bigger ship. It was either on autopilot, or—more likely—the helmsman was half asleep.

Then the radio exploded into life with a furious barrage of shouts. Somebody had obviously woken up to what was happening. The Maestro grinned, but made no attempt to reply.

Ernesto held his course. Big Pig Island was looming up out of the darkness, its high cliffs and ruined buildings lit by the flashes from the light-house. It looked like something out of a Dracula movie.

They were almost there!

The captain of the freighter had abandoned his radio now, and was out on the wing bridge, raining curses down on them—his voice rising to a crescendo of fury and disbelief as the two ships narrowly avoided collision. Judging by his accent he was from India. The Maestro gave him a cheerful wave, then ignored him completely.

They were approaching the western side of the island, its cliffs soaring into the night sky. Somewhere above them was the gun platform where Jik had done his amazing dance before he'd led the Sea Wolf to the wild pigs' lair.

They held their course until the last moment. Then the Maestro issued a curt order, and *The Dreamboat* slowed. The freighter churned past and disappeared, its captain shaking his fist at them as it went.

Ernesto spun the wheel, and they crept in towards shore, a crewman in the bows dropping a weighted line into the water, calling out the depths as they went. It must have been like this centuries ago, Hanna thought, when old-time pirates mounted raids on island strongholds. She felt a shiver of anticipation—or was it fear?—as the anchor splashed down close to the base of the cliffs, and the ancient ship swung to a halt.

Had they been seen? It was impossible to tell.

To be safe, they waited what seemed like an age before they made any move. Then the dive boats were lowered into the water.

They would split into two groups. The Maestro would take one boat, and go with Hanna and Ned and four crewmen round to the far side of the island. A second group of crewmen, with Jik as guide, would take another, and land as close as possible to where they were now anchored. With luck—and if everything went to plan—they would eventually meet in the middle. Ernesto would stay with Nina and the dive boys to guard the ship.

Before they left, everybody gathered on the foredeck, heads bowed, whilst Nina recited prayers to the Blessed Santo Nino. While they were praying, Hanna glanced at the crewmen. They looked exactly like they had a year earlier, when they'd come ashore on Kaitan to kidnap Mum and Dad—bandannas wound round their heads, razor-sharp parangs hanging from their waists. Had they said prayers to Santo Nino that night too? It was a disturbing thought.

The Maestro's party left first. At the last moment, Nina bustled across with a cup of medicine and thrust it at her brother. She forced him to drink a small amount—it would help him to stay calm, she told him. Then she embraced him, and he followed Hanna and Ned down the ship's side into the biggest of the dive boats. The four crewmen joined them. Oars were unshipped, and they moved silently away into the night.

Despite the distance they had to travel—round the northern tip of the island, and down the rocky east coast—rowing was their only option. The noise from an engine would have given them away immediately. But there was no complaint from the crewmen, even when the boat began to buck and pitch as they hit the swell from the South China Sea, soaking everybody on board with spray.

It took them almost two hours of hard rowing to reach the hidden cove where the big black inflatables were kept. As they approached it, Hanna became aware of her heart beating painfully. Dozens of lives depended on their plan working perfectly. Suddenly there seemed to be so much that could go wrong!

There was a tiny inlet close to the entrance to the cove, visible only from the sea. The Maestro steered the boat into it, and ran it up onto the beach.

'You OK?' he whispered to the children, as they scrambled out.

They nodded. The crewmen signalled that they were ready too. They adjusted their *parangs* and slipped into the water. Hanna, Ned, and the Maestro waded in to join them.

It was time to swim.

Hanna had been concerned that the current might be against them, but after two or three strokes she relaxed. The tide was coming in quickly, sweeping them round into the cove. As planned, she and Ned took the lead, with the Maestro and his men fanned out behind them. They swam breast-stroke to avoid splashes that might be noticed from the shore.

After a few minutes, the beach with its concrete slipway came into view. To the children's relief, the two black boats were sitting in their shallow cave. That meant the Sea Wolf and his men were back inside their underground lair, no doubt planning more murderous pirate attacks. Hanna allowed herself a smile. If everything went to plan, they were in for a very nasty shock!

She glanced back at the Maestro and his men. One moment they were there; the next moment, with scarcely a ripple to mark where they'd dived, they were gone. There was no going back now! 'Ready, Ned?' she whispered.

He nodded; shot her an affectionate grin. His face was silver in the moonlight. What a brilliant brother he was, Hanna thought, as she raised her arms above her head and began to wave them frantically in the air.

Pretending to drown was no problem at all!

Splashing and shouting, the two children floundered onto the beach. Hanna hauled herself a few feet above the water line, then 'collapsed' face down onto the sand. Ned, meanwhile, staggered to his feet and lurched off in the direction of the boat cave, coughing and spluttering. *'Help!'* he was yelling. *'Help! My sister's drowned!'*

After making sure he'd been clearly seen by the security cameras, he stumbled back to Hanna and flopped down—apparently unconscious—on top of her. He was being a little too realistic, she thought ruefully, as she struggled to get back the breath that he'd knocked out of her body.

For what seemed an age, but can have only been a few seconds, nothing happened. Then came the sound of running feet. Torches flicked on, their powerful beams sweeping the beach. Out of the corner of her eye Hanna saw two armed guards hurrying towards them. They were shouting to each other in Malay, clearly alarmed.

'You're dead, remember,' Ned whispered. 'Go really floppy!'

Hanna flopped.

Hands gripped them, turned them over. There was a gasp of fear. These were the same guards who'd left the children in the galley of the *Ocean Spur*, apparently sliced to pieces and covered with blood! They bent to take a closer look, unable to believe their eyes.

It was the last move they made.

The Maestro and his men rose silently out of the water behind them. There were dull thuds as heavy ironwood clubs, normally used to stun fish, descended onto the backs of their heads. They slumped down, unconscious.

Instantly, Hanna and Ned scrambled to their feet. There was no time to lose!

Jon-Jon, the crewman who normally looked after *The Dreamboat's* engine, sprinted towards the tractor, which was parked next to the inflatables. It roared into life. One after the other, the huge boats were hauled out onto the beach and pushed into the tunnel that led to the Sea Wolf's headquarters. *Parangs* rose and fell, slashing through their thick rubber casings. They collapsed with a loud hiss.

The rest of the crewmen, helped by Hanna and Ned, hurried to fetch drums of fuel. These were emptied onto the deflated boats.

There were shouts from inside the tunnel, the shrilling of an alarm. A shot whistled out of the darkness and clanged off the metal cowling of the tractor.

The men ignored it.

The entrance to the tunnel was supported by

two stout timbers. A chain was swiftly looped round them and attached to the tractor. Jon-Jon revved the engine. *'Go!'* yelled the Maestro.

The tractor accelerated hard. The chain tightened, and the supports were wrenched away.

At the very last moment, the Maestro took a lighter from a waterproof bag on his belt, lit an oily rag and threw it onto the fuel-soaked boats. There was a gush of flame, immediately followed by clouds of thick black smoke as the rubber caught fire.

Then he sprinted to safety as the entrance to the tunnel collapsed.

Hanna glanced at Ned, exhilarated. Within minutes the flames from the boats would spread to the stacks of old motor tyres stored in the chambers on either side of the tunnel. They'd burn for hours, filling the whole of the Sea Wolf's underground headquarters with smoke. Nobody would be able to stay inside. What a plan! So far it was working brilliantly.

There was a narrow path up the cliff face on the far side of the cove. Hanna had spotted it when they'd been hiding in the boat lockers before the raid on the *Ocean Spur*. She prayed it went all the way to the top. She pointed at it. 'Let's go!' she yelled.

There was no need for caution now—only speed

254

mattered. Grabbing the guns from the unconscious guards, the Maestro and his men followed the children as they scrambled rapidly upwards, away from the beach.

It took longer than Hanna had expected to climb the cliffs—in places the path had fallen away, and they had to move cautiously from handhold to handhold. But eventually they made it. Wading through chest-high elephant grass they headed towards the ruined parade ground in the centre of the island. Hanna hoped there were no angry pigs anywhere close by.

As they emerged onto the rubble-strewn square an extraordinary sight met their eyes. *The Dreamboat*'s biggest fishing net had been spread out across the ground and weighted down with heavy slabs of fallen masonry. Beneath it was the trapdoor that led to the Sea Wolf's headquarters.

Jik and the crewmen were standing round the net staring at it expectantly. Hanna caught the Sea Gypsy boy's eye as she arrived. She smiled. He smiled back her. He was loving every minute of it. Ned, who'd raced across to join his friend, was doing an excited dance at his side.

Any minute now the fish would be caught!

There was a sudden loud thumping from beneath the trapdoor, and it swung open. Black smoke belched out. Coughing and spluttering, the Sea Wolf's men began to emerge.

They had no chance to escape. Before they'd even had time to draw a breath, the crewmen were onto them, rolling them up in the net, lashing them into tight bundles with rope.

In little more than a minute, seven . . . eight . . . *nine* men were caught and trussed up. In the darkness they looked like black, wriggling pigs.

Easy peasy! Now for the rest of them!

The children waited expectantly. The smoke was getting thicker by the second, pumping up into the moonlit sky. Surely they must come out soon!

They didn't.

Hanna's elation faded, to be replaced by a growing anxiety. She was certain there were several people still underground—including the Sea Wolf. She remembered Mum telling her that more people were killed by breathing in smoke than were ever burnt to death in house fires. Could this be happening to them?

Her question was answered moments later. A harsh shout rang out from behind her: *'Drop your guns! Put your hands up!'*

She spun on her heels. Emerging from the ruined buildings were four of the Sea Wolf's men, led by Hawk-Nose. They had semi-automatic rifles levelled. There was obviously another exit from the underground warren that the children didn't know about!

'Are you deaf! Do what you're told!'

The Maestro and Jon-Jon, who were holding the guards' rifles, put them down slowly. The Maestro, Hanna saw, had become dangerously purple in the face. As she raised her hands above her head, she prayed that Nina's medicine would continue to work. One false move and they'd all be dead.

'Get over there!' Hawk-Nose snarled, indicating a nearby wall. *'Line up!'*

The children were grabbed, shoved hard against the crumbling brickwork. The Maestro and his men were hustled across to join them.

For a second or two Hanna was puzzled. Why were they being made to line up?

Then she understood.

They were going to be executed—gunned down in cold blood.

Trembling with shock, she groped for the boys' hands. There could be no escape this time. It was over. They turned to face their killers.

The gunmen took aim, their weapons gleaming in the moonlight. There were going to be no last words. No final requests.

Hawk-Nose raised his arm to give the signal to fire . . .

And staggered back, clutching his left eye.

Blood was pumping out of it, gushing through his fingers. He let out a howl of agony.

The gunmen swung towards him in alarm. Then it was their turn to scream as a barrage of viciously-aimed pebbles smashed into them. They dropped their guns and sank to their knees, clutching broken teeth, blinded eyes, crushed noses, as one by one their faces were battered to a bloody pulp.

Hawk-Nose tried to reach for his gun, but he was felled by a second salvo of shots. He pitched forward, and was still.

There was a shout of glee, and suddenly the whole parade ground was full of ecstatic dive boys, clutching catapults, racing about, giving each other high fives, pausing occasionally to fire yet more pebbles into the cowering bodies of the gunmen. Eventually, Hanna had to yell at them to stop. Any more shots from close range and the men would be dead. She didn't want anybody to die. That would make them all no better than the Sea Wolf.

The Maestro and his men grabbed the gunmen, swiftly tied them up in the fishing net, and dumped them on top of the others.

Hanna's brain was reeling. It had all happened so fast! The dive boys had been no part of the plan—they'd been told to stay on board *The*

Dreamboat and stay quiet. They must have jumped overboard and swum to the shore, anxious to help. Thank goodness they'd disobeyed their orders! She caught Kalbo's eye. He was the oldest of the boys and the best shot with a catapult. It was his idea, she was sure of it.

She tried to tell him how amazing he was—how amazing all the boys were—but he was no longer looking at her. He was pointing over her shoulder. 'Man!' he exclaimed. 'I see man!'

Hanna spun round.

At first she could see nothing. But then, in the distance, she spotted a flash of white. Somebody was dodging between the ruined buildings, moving swiftly towards the northern tip of the island.

The flash of white came from a bandage.

It was the Sea Wolf!

The others had spotted him too. Leaving Jon-Jon to guard the captives, the Maestro set off in frantic pursuit. The rest followed. There was no way they were going to let the evil Sea Wolf escape now!

It was like a crazy obstacle race, with men and boys dodging in and out of buildings, crashing through stands of elephant grass, yelling at the tops of their voices. The Sea Wolf had almost reached the ruined chapel that marked the northern point of the island now. He seemed to be making no attempt to hide himself as he ran. Why was he going there? Hanna wondered. There was nothing beyond it except a sheer cliff dropping hundreds of metres down to the sea below. Unless he could fly, he'd be trapped for certain.

It was almost as if he was *willing* them to follow him.

Her chest heaving with the effort, she caught up with Ned and Jik, who'd sped on ahead. As she did so, a shot rang out. The bullet ricocheted off one of the ruined buildings and whined away into the darkness.

The Sea Wolf had taken out a pistol and was firing at them.

A second shot followed. And a third.

As everybody dived for cover, there was an answering burst of gunfire from one of the crewmen, followed by more shots from the Sea Wolf.

The gun-battle had hardly begun, before it was over. The Maestro grabbed the crewman's rifle, and hurled it away from him. 'No shooting!' he yelled. 'I kill him with my bare hands!'

The Sea Wolf tried a final shot but his gun was empty.

'*Come on!*' yelled Jik, breathless with excitement. '*Let's get him!*'

The children expected the Sea Wolf to try to

escape, but he didn't. He stopped, turned to face them. He reached into his pocket and took something out.

It was a remote control unit. He was pointing it away to his left. Puzzled, they followed the direction of his hand.

A red light glowed in the darkness.

What on earth could it be?

At that moment the moon came out from behind a cloud, and to her horror, Hanna saw what it was.

It was a detonator—and it was fixed to the nose of the huge unexploded bomb they'd seen that day when they'd followed Jik to the ruined chapel to 'pray'. The Sea Wolf had only to press a button and they'd all be blown to pieces!

'Get down!' she screamed.

The boys and the crewmen had spotted the bomb too. They flung themselves flat, hands covering their ears.

There was a burst of laughter from the Sea Wolf. He was challenging them—taunting them. 'Not so brave now, are you? Still want to come and get me! No, of course you don't! That's because you're cowards! I spit on you!'

He was inching slowly backwards towards the edge of the cliff, his hand still outstretched, his finger pressed to the remote control button. Was he intending to commit suicide and take them all with him?

A furious shout split the air. It was the Maestro. The Sea Wolf's taunts had obviously struck home. His face was distorted with rage. He lurched to his feet, foam bubbling from his lips. '*I kill you!*' he roared. '*I kill you! I break your neck!*'

'Back off!' the Sea Wolf warned. 'I'll press this button!'

It was too late. The Maestro was beyond any sort of understanding now. He stumbled forwards, pounding his huge fists together. '*I kill you!*'

Suddenly Hanna knew what she had to do. Kalbo was lying next to her clutching his catapult. 'Stop him!' she ordered, pointing at the Maestro. 'Stop him now!'

Kalbo stared at her in panic. 'Cannot . . . '

'*Now! If not he'll get us all blown to pieces!*'

The boy took a deep breath, plucked up courage and leapt to his feet. He drew back his catapult and fired.

The stone cracked against the Maestro's left temple. He shook his head once, as if he couldn't believe what had happened, then pitched forward, unconscious.

There was a stunned silence. Hanna grabbed at Kalbo, desperately trying to make him lie down again; but he shook her off and fired a second shot.

It was as accurate as his first. But this time his target was the remote control unit in the Sea Wolf's hands. It disintegrated into a mess of shattered plastic and flying batteries. The red light on the detonator went out.

With a deafening yell, the men and boys rose to their feet and charged. For an instant it looked as if the Sea Wolf would stay and fight, but then he turned, and without a backwards glance, leapt over the cliff.

Followed by the others, Hanna sprinted to the edge and stared downwards.

She gasped in surprise. Instead of plunging to his death onto the rocks below, the Sea Wolf had grabbed an overhead pulley, and was sailing smoothly down a stout metal cable.

It was a zip wire!

At the bottom of it, moored to a rock, was a small inflatable boat with a powerful engine. His escape route had obviously been meticulously planned.

The boys tried to hit him with their catapults, but the range was already too long. Then somebody grabbed a gun and started to fire.

'*Stop!*' yelled Ned frantically. He was pointing downwards.

Two figures had stepped out of the shadow of the rocks below. One was a man—short and round. The other was a woman. She was immensely fat, wearing a bright pink blouse and a pair of glittering diamanté earrings.

They were both holding stout wooden clubs.

The Sea Wolf was halfway down the cliff-face when he spotted them. He bellowed with rage, but there was nothing he could do. Zip wires don't have brakes.

As the dive-boys and the crewmen yelled their encouragement from above, Nina and Ernesto positioned themselves, legs apart, at the bottom of the wire, swung back their clubs and waited . . .

30
The Moon Pearl

It was like something out of a war film. The helicopters came in fast and low from the east, hugging the waves before zooming up above the steep cliffs of Big Pig Island. Two of them hovered, with machine-guns aimed downwards at the parade ground, while a third came in to land.

The moment it touched down, armed soldiers were tumbling out of it, racing for cover amongst the ruined buildings.

Motioning to Nina to keep everybody out of sight in the long grass, Hanna borrowed Ned's shirt. It had been white originally, but was now a dirty grey colour. She hoped it would do. She stuck it on the end of a stick, gave the boys an encouraging smile. 'Ready?'

They nodded.

'OK. Let's stand up slowly. We mustn't give them any excuse to start shooting.'

It was late the following afternoon, and everything should have been sorted out long ago. But there'd been confusion and disbelief when they'd finally got through to the Philippine authorities on *The Dreamboat*'s crackling radio. How much had been understood? Not a lot, it seemed. It would be ironic if their rescuers turned out to be more dangerous than the Sea Wolf and his men!

Waving the flag, smiling in what they hoped was a reassuring way, the three children got to their feet and walked slowly towards the helicopter.

'Hello! It's us!' Ned shouted. *'It's Ned and Hanna and Jik—'*

He didn't finish. All three of them were seized from behind, thrust face downwards onto the cracked concrete of the parade ground. Rough hands frisked them for weapons before they were hauled back to their feet.

A young officer approached them. 'I'm Major Cervantes,' he said. 'Where are the pirates?'

There was a squeal of pain from the long grass. One of the soldiers emerged holding Kalbo by the ear. 'I find one, sir!'

'No, you've got it wrong!' Hanna said desperately. 'He's not a pirate! He's just a boy. He's one of our friends.'

'So where *are* the pirates?'

'Locked up. On our ship.'

Major Cervantes looked disbelieving. 'All of them?'

'All of them.'

'We catch every dam one of them!' Jik exclaimed. 'We are amazing! We are wonderful!'

'Jik,' said Hanna, beginning to relax a little, 'put a sock in it!'

'I got no goddam sock!' the Sea Gypsy boy complained. He looked at Ned and giggled.

Finally the major seemed to get the message. He spoke quickly into his radio and the two remaining helicopters dropped down to land next to the first one.

As their engines cut, more soldiers leapt out, followed, after a short delay, by four familiar figures in civilian clothes.

It was Mum and Dad!

And Jik's Mum and Dad!

Hurdling lumps of masonry, the children raced towards their parents and flung themselves into their arms.

Everybody was crying—even Dad. Hanna had never seen him cry before and it made her own tears come even faster. The anxiety and stress they'd suffered was etched deep into their careworn, loving faces.

But then anger began to surface. *'You promised me!'* Mum said quietly, accusingly.

Hanna glanced at Ned and Jik. It was *their* fault, not hers! She hadn't known anything about their stupid plan to find the Moon Pearl until it was too late to do anything about it! She was about to tell Mum so when she stopped herself. They were a *team*—she and Jik and Ned. The best team on the planet! They'd been through hell together and come out the other side. There was no way she was going to get them into extra trouble now.

'It was a mistake,' she said softly.

Now Dad's anger began to flare. 'Some mistake! Do you have any idea what we've been through—what Jik's mum and dad have been through?'

Hanna tried to answer, but Dad was no longer listening to her. His gaze had switched to the thick grass beyond the perimeter of the parade ground. Emerging from it, looking hesitant and apprehensive, were the dive boys and the crewmen. Behind them, urging them onwards, was Nina. The Maestro stumbled along beside her, his hands clasped to his head. They looked like survivors from a war.

Dad peered at them closely. As he did so, his expression changed. 'It's them!' he roared. 'It's the pirates who tried to kill us last year! I'll never forget their faces!' He twisted towards Major Cervantes. 'Arrest them now! They're murderers!'

'No, Dad!' Ned yelled, grabbing his father. 'You don't understand! They're not murderers! They're just ordinary people like you and me and Hanna and Mum!'

Dad broke away. He went up close to the Maestro, stared into his scarred, dirt-smeared face. For one horrible moment Hanna thought Dad was going to punch him.

'Please, Dad, listen to us!' she pleaded.

It was Mum who came to the rescue. She went over to Dad, took his arm. 'I think you should listen to what the children have got to say, Nick,' she said softly. 'I think we should all listen and not jump to conclusions.'

It took a long time to tell their story—a very long time. Everybody gathered round to hear it, including the soldiers.

'That's the most extraordinary thing I've ever heard,' Dad said, when the children had finally finished.

'But it's goddam true!' Jik—who'd been translating for the benefit of his parents—emphasized.

'And all the time we thought this Sea Wolf was *protecting* ships!' Major Cervantes exclaimed. 'He made fools of us.'

'He made fools of everybody,' Hanna said.

There was a sudden noise from the major's radio. He answered it. 'The navy ship will be here in a few minutes,' he announced. 'We must supervise the transfer of prisoners.'

Everybody gathered on the old gun platform to watch, as a sleek patrol vessel slid in next to *The Dreamboat* and tied up alongside. Jon-Jon and Ernesto, who'd been guarding the prisoners, stood back as a squad of armed soldiers came on board and disappeared into the hold.

Moments later they began to emerge with the Sea Wolf's men.

They were a sorry sight—heavily bandaged and smoke-blackened. They were frog-marched rapidly onto the navy vessel and taken down to the cells below.

One of the last to be brought up was the Sea Wolf. He was sporting two large black eyes—courtesy of Nina and Ernesto—and his limp was even more pronounced. He glared up at the children. *'I'm not finished yet!'* he snarled. *'One day you'll pay for this—all of you!'*

He was going to say more, but he was jerked away out of sight.

It was over.

But not quite.

As the children turned away, already dreaming of a slap-up meal and a comfortable bed, they found Dad standing in front of them, his arms folded. 'Well?' he said.

'Well what?' Hanna asked.

'Are we just going to go home and leave it here? After everything that's happened?'

'Leave *what* here?'

Ned didn't wait for Dad's reply. Nor did Jik. *'The Moon Pearl!'* they both yelled at the same time. *'We've forgotten about the Moon Pearl!'*

Instantly their tiredness disappeared. 'So where is it?' Ned demanded. 'Only you know, Jik! Come on, tell us!'

Jik put on a mysterious expression. ' Manai Liha say, *Muchia Bulan*—the Moon Pearl—is buried where the chicken lays its egg.'

'What on earth did she mean by that?' Hanna asked, puzzled.

Jik spread his hands. 'Holy Moses, I don't know!'

'There are no chickens on this island!' Ned exclaimed. 'Only wild pigs.'

Suddenly one of the dive boys piped up. It was Jun, the youngest. He knew a few words of English. 'I see chicken!' he said excitedly. 'I see it when I go to shoot with my *lastic*. Come! Quick!'

Beckoning everybody to follow him, he raced to the centre of the island. He stopped at an outcrop of bare limestone rock that the children had passed several times before. He pointed, and made a clucking noise.

Mystified, the children stared at where he was

indicating. It was just a load of rocks. 'I can't see anything,' Hanna said.

Jun reached for her hand and pulled her a few metres to the left.

As he did so, the rocks seemed to form themselves into the shape of a chicken—a very *large* chicken—with a round hole where its bottom ought to be!

Excited, she called the boys over. 'What do we do now?' Ned asked, staring at it perplexed.

'Wait for it to lay goddam egg,' Jik told him. 'Remember I tell you the Moon Pearl is buried where the first ray of moonlight touches the ground?'

'Yes. But I don't see what that's got to do with a stone chicken with a hole in its bum!'

'You wait, see.'

Dusk was falling rapidly. As everybody watched and waited, a full moon slowly rose above the eastern rim of the island. Its light was masked by the rocks, except in one place—the hole in the 'chicken's' bottom.

Through it shone a shaft of pure silver light. It fell on the ground close to where Hanna was standing, forming a perfect oval shape.

The chicken had laid its egg!

'Let's dig!' yelled Ned, leaping up and down in excitement.

The soldiers ran to fetch shovels and torches from the helicopters. It took only a few minutes' digging before one of them announced: 'I find box!'

The children crowded round as he lifted it out carefully. It was a stout wooden casket, bound with rusted iron bands. He broke open the locks with the tip of his spade.

He beckoned Jik forwards. The Sea Gypsy boy lifted the lid gingerly.

Inside was a round object—about the size of a small football—wrapped in oiled silk.

Hanna held her breath. She could only imagine how beautiful—how *lustrous*—the giant pearl was going to be. It would shine brighter than the moon itself! Her whole body was tingling with excitement.

With shaking hands Jik began to unwrap it. The oiled silk fell away.

There was a loud gasp from everybody watching.

What Jik was holding may or may not have been the biggest pearl in the world.

But it was certainly the ugliest!

It wasn't even properly round—it was covered with knobs and bumps like a potato. And instead of a lustrous sheen, its surface was chalky-white, and covered with splits and cracks.

As the children stared at it, stunned, Dad came over and examined it closely. 'I'm afraid it's worthless,' he said, sounding as disappointed as they were, 'except maybe as a museum piece. It's just an ugly lump of calcium. I can't imagine why anybody would want to bury it in the first place.'

'But we were going to be rich!' Ned wailed. 'We were going to be millionaires!'

Mum came up to him, looped an arm round his shoulders, hugged him to her. 'I think we're already rich enough, Ned,' she said softly. 'We're all safe and well—and thanks to you three, and the brave people on *The Dreamboat*, some of the most evil people on this planet are behind bars—hopefully for good.'

'Praise be to the blessed Santo Nino, you are right!' Nina exclaimed, breaking into a huge smile. 'Now we can *all* go home!'

31

Holy Moses!

Late October, and it had been raining all day. As Hanna and Ned trooped out of school and headed for the bus stop, Borneo seemed a million miles away. 'Had a good day?' Hanna asked Ned as he trailed along behind her.

'Nah!'

'Me neither. And I've got stacks of homework.'

'Me too!'

There was a swish of tyres and a van drew up next to them. It was Dad! He leant across and opened the passenger door. 'Thought you guys might like to go to the White Lion for tea,' he said.

The children climbed in mystified. Dad *never* took them for tea, and he *never* picked them up from school—except on very special occasions.

Was *this* a special occasion?

The White Lion was a hotel in the High Street and it was quite posh. The children ordered fruit smoothies and big slices of chocolate cake. Dad settled for a cup of tea.

When the waitress had gone, he smiled and said, 'I've got some good news and some good news. Which would you like to hear first?'

'The good news!' chorused Hanna and Ned.

'OK. Your grandfather in Malaysia is much better, so Mum's coming home!'

The restaurant was full of old ladies. Their heads swivelled as Hanna's and Ned's cheers rang out. It had been *so* difficult leaving Mum behind when they'd flown home after their amazing adventure in the summer. But she'd told them her father needed her more than they did, and had insisted on staying behind. Mum would arrive back on Saturday, Dad said, and they'd all go to meet her at Heathrow.

He paused. Then he said, 'I've got some more good news too. I've had a call from our lawyer in the Philippines. The trial of the Sea Wolf and his men ended yesterday. They've been found guilty and sentenced to life imprisonment—with no chance of their ever being released.'

Ned started to cheer again, but Hanna cut him short. 'What about Pepe,' she asked anxiously. 'What about the cook? He saved our lives!'

Dad smiled. 'Don't worry! Your statement was read out in court. He's been given a suspended sentence, which means he's free to go home to his wife and children.'

'Thank goodness for that,' Hanna said, relieved.

'There's more.'

'More?'

'It seems the Sea Wolf was linked to a group of crooked ship owners from across the globe. You probably wondered why his men sank the *Ocean Spur* after all its oil had been stolen?'

Hanna and Ned nodded.

'That was so its owners could claim the insurance money—not just for its cargo, which they'd already sold to the Chinese—but for the ship itself, which was insured for far more than it was worth and would be reported lost at sea. The Sea Wolf and his friends were part of a multi-million pound crime syndicate, which—thanks to you—has finally been smashed.' Dad eyed them keenly. 'That means you qualify for the reward.'

'Reward?' chorused the children, their eyes like saucers.

The old ladies' heads swivelled again.

'I've known about the reward for some time, but it was dependent on how the Sea Wolf's trial went. So I didn't tell you in case you got disappointed. It's being paid out by the insurance companies and it's quite a lot of money.'

Hanna began to tremble. 'How much money?' she just managed to ask.

'Half a million pounds.'

'Half a million pounds!' yelled the children.

Yet again the old ladies swivelled. It was the most exciting afternoon they'd had in years.

'We're rich!' Ned said, his eyes glowing. *'Stinking* rich!'

Dad held up his hands. 'Not so fast! I've been in touch with Jik's dad. We've decided that most of it will go to Nina. She'll use it to buy an ocean-going trawler, so they can stop diving on the reefs, destroying the coral, and fish further out to sea. They'll use the profits from their catches to rebuild their village. There should be enough left over to provide homes for the dive boys, and put them through school. It will also pay for a trip to New York for the Maestro to have brain surgery. His chances of making a complete recovery are quite good, so I'm told.'

'So *we* don't get anything?' Ned said plaintively.

Hanna glared at him. 'It doesn't matter,' she said crossly. 'Like Mum said, we've got everything we need.'

Dad smiled. 'Actually, you'll get several thousand pounds each, which Mum and I are going to put into a trust fund for when you're older.'

'What about Jik?' Ned asked.

'He'll get the same amount as you. I've had a

long talk with Jik's dad. He wants to use Jik's share for his education.'

'So he'll go to school in America?'

Dad smiled again. 'Maybe. But while we were discussing it I had a crazy idea. How about if he comes to England and goes to your school?'

'Our school!'

'He can stay with us during term time and go home for the holidays. Of course you'll have to share a room, Ned.'

Ned leapt to his feet and began to do his frantic dance, much to the astonishment of the old ladies. 'Wicked!' he yelled, waving his arms in the air. 'Not just wicked—*mega* wicked! We're going to have *so* much fun!'

Hanna groaned. '*Holy Moses!*' was all she managed to say.

David Miller was born in Norfolk. He has worked in advertising for most of his career, as a copy-writer, and later as a creative director.

He has travelled widely all over the world, and lived and worked in Malaysia and Singapore for more than ten years. *Sea Wolf* is his second novel for children. Like his first, *Shark Island*, it is set in the wild Sulu Sea, north of Borneo, and was inspired by actual events.

David now writes full-time, and lives in Hampshire with his wife Su'en and his daughter Hanna.

LEOPARD'S CLAW

1

Rough Justice

'Nicholas James Bailey, you have been found guilty of first degree murder. You will be executed by firing squad four weeks from this date, at a location yet to be decided . . . '

Dad flinched, as if every badly-pronounced word the judge read out was a bullet slamming into his body. His knees began to buckle. Only the prison guards holding on to him stopped him from collapsing entirely.

For a moment there was silence. Then the crowd in Court One of the Sangabera Justice Building erupted. People who, seconds earlier, had been sitting quietly, leapt to their feet as if under orders, and began to shout, waving their arms in the air. For an instant, Mum was lost in the crush. But then the children saw her launch herself from her seat and throw herself at the judge.

'You can't do this!' she screamed. 'You've got no proof! He's innocent!'

A court official tried to stop her, but she shoved him aside. Mum—quiet, kind, sensible Mum had turned into a ferocious beast. She reached the judges' table and climbed on to it, lashing out at anybody who tried to restrain her. She grabbed the judge by the collar of his scarlet and black robe, thrust her face close to his.

'Take back what you just said!' she yelled. 'Take it back! You know he's innocent. This isn't justice!'

Panic-stricken, Hanna, Ned and Jik tried to get to her—but there were too many people in the way. Alarm bells shrilled. Armed police, batons raised, burst into the courtroom. Mum was grabbed by the neck. Other policemen seized Dad, thrusting his arms hard up behind his back, making him shout out in agony. The judge and his two assistants picked up their papers and scurried out of a side exit.

'That's my mum!' Ned was screaming, wrestling with anybody in his way as he fought to reach her. 'Take your hands off my mum!'

Hanna was fighting too. She managed to get to Dad and hold onto him. For a split second their eyes met. He was saying something to her, she realised—repeating the same two words over and over again. But what were they? It was impossible to tell with all the shouting and screaming. She tried to get him to speak louder, but a baton descended painfully on her arm and her grip was broken. She watched helplessly as he was dragged out of the court and thrust into a waiting police van. Mum was carried out after him and thrown kicking into a second van. Sirens howling, the vehicles accelerated away.

The crowd was growing by the minute as more and more people arrived, attracted by the noise. With Mum and Dad gone, their attention turned to the children.

'Anak kriminal!' they were screaming. 'Anak kriminal!'

Hanna knew enough Indonesian to understand what they were saying. They were accusing the three of them of being criminals—child criminals. Punches were thrown. Jik, the Sea Gypsy boy, let out a yelp of pain as a fist caught him in the mouth, making the blood flow. 'We go!' he yelled at Hanna and Ned, fighting to get away. 'We go now!'

Fresh police charged into the courtroom, batons flailing. A gap opened up behind them. Seizing their chance, the children dashed for the door.

They reached it, and were through. Three men had spotted them, and were giving chase. Dodging flowerpots and benches, the Hanna, Ned and Jik sprinted through the open doors of the court building and out into the sunlit street of the East Borneo capital. One of their pursuers soon gave up—but the other two were young and fit.

'Anak kriminal!' they were screaming, their faces distorted with hatred. They were catching up fast.

There was a warung—a small eating-house—opposite. Jik, who was in the lead, dodged into it. Hanna and Ned followed him. The diners looked up from their food in surprise, as the three children dashed through, scattering chairs, heading for the kitchen. The owner, a thin man with bad teeth, was stir-frying something in a wok. He snarled angrily as they barged past him and into the alley behind the shop.

Their pursuers were close behind, but they were large men, and the kitchen was tiny. There was a cry of pain. One of them had collided with the wok and had splashed himself with hot cooking oil. His companion stopped to help him.

It was the chance the children had been waiting for. They raced along the alley at high speed. Up ahead was a main road. If they could reach it in time, they could maybe disappear into the crowd and get away.

But there were police sirens, getting louder by the second. They seemed to be coming from all directions at once.

On one side of the alley was a deep storm drain. It was half full of water and floating garbage. It ran underneath the main road in a tunnel and came out on the other side. Jik pointed at it. 'We go in there!' he yelled.

Hanna opened her mouth to protest, but she was too late. The Sea Gypsy boy leapt into the drain. The slimy black water came up to his knees. He disappeared from sight underneath the road.

Ned was next.

Holding her nose, Hanna followed.

She was just in time. A powerful police motorcycle had turned into the alleyway and was speeding towards them. Praying that they hadn't been spotted, she waded quickly towards the boys.

They waited in the gloom, holding their breaths. The motor bike roared to a halt above their heads. A police car, its siren wailing, drew up next to it. They heard voices.

'What are they saying?' Hanna asked Jik.

'They're asking if anybody has seen the criminals.'

'We're not criminals!' Ned protested loudly.

'Quiet!' Jik ordered. 'Or they goddam hear you!'

More cars pulled up. It was as if the entire Indonesian police force had decided to hold a rally right above their heads. Surely somebody must think of looking into the drain beneath their feet?

Nobody did. After a few minutes, doors slammed, engines started up, and the vehicles roared off.

Silence fell. Trembling with shock, Hanna peered around her. Floating nearby was what looked like an old sack.

It wasn't.

It was a dog. It had obviously been dead for a long time. Most of its fur was missing, and its swollen belly was split open like an over-stuffed cushion. Where its intestines had once been was a writhing mass of maggots.

'We've got to get out of here,' she gasped. 'We'll catch a disease.'

She turned to go, but Jik grabbed her. 'Wait,' he hissed. 'Maybe there is still a policeman up there. Maybe they play a dam trick to make us think they have all gone.'

'But this is horrible!' Ned protested.

'Better than go to goddam jail!'

They forced themselves to stand still and wait. There was a gentle current and to Hanna's horror, the dead dog began to drift towards her. She felt it bump softly—slimily—against her bare legs.

She tried to push it away, but it came back again. And again.

'I don't care if there are policemen up there!' she exclaimed, unable to stand any more. 'I'm not staying here a moment longer!'

Her words were drowned by a violent clap of thunder.

A tropical storm, which had been building all morning, was breaking above their heads. As lightning flashed, rain began to cascade from the sky, drumming on the hard surface of the road, sluicing into the culverts.

Within seconds the water level inside the drain had risen to chest height. They had to get out of their hiding place fast!

Half walking, half-swimming, terrified of slipping and being swept away, the children staggered towards the light. They were just in time. As the water hit the top of the tunnel, filling it completely, they pulled themselves clear, and lay gasping on the concrete surround. The dead dog shot past after them, shedding maggots like passengers from a sinking ship. It surged away down the drain and out of sight.

They stayed where they were for long time, not moving, letting the rain wash the filth from their bodies. There were all sorts of diseases you could catch from dirty water, Hanna knew—typhoid, cholera. She prayed that nobody had swallowed any.

The storm ended as quickly as it had begun, and the sun came out. The three children pulled themselves slowly to their feet, not knowing what to do next. As they did so, a voice made them freeze.

'Like drowned rats,' it said. 'Like three drowned rats!'

They spun on their heels. A man was squatting in a nearby doorway. He was young—in his late twenties it looked like—wearing jeans and a faded black T-shirt. His hair was scraped back into a tight ponytail. He grinned at them, then glanced downwards into his lap.

He was cradling a long-barrelled handgun.